"Goir

Hannah ___, ___ ___ pulled away from the curb and mainstreamed into the San Francisco traffic. That voice. She knew that voice.

e couldn't look up, her eyes still set on her phone. She curled her fingers more tightly around the heavy fabric of her wedding gown as she took a breath and raised her gaze, locking with dark, nse eyes in the rearview mirror.

knew those eyes too. No one had eyes like . They seemed to cut through you, possessing ability to read your innermost secrets. Able nock and flirt in a single glance. She still saw se eyes in her dreams. And sometimes in her htmares.

iardo Vega. One of the many skeletons in her set. Except he wasn't staying put.

Maisey Yates was an avid Mills & Boon® Modern™ Romance reader before she began to write them. She still can't quite believe she's lucky enough to get to create her very own sexy alpha heroes and feisty heroines. Seeing her name on one of those lovely covers is a dream come true.

Maisey lives with her handsome, wonderful, diaper-changing husband and three small children across the street from her extremely supportive parents and the home she grew up in, in the wilds of Southern Oregon, USA. She enjoys the contrast of living in a place where you might wake up to find a bear on your back porch and then heading into the home office to write stories that take place in exotic urban locales.

Recent titles by the same author:

A ROYAL WORLD APART
ONE NIGHT IN PARADISE
GIRL ON A DIAMOND PEDESTAL
HAJAR'S HIDDEN LEGACY

A GAME OF VOWS

BY
MAISEY YATES

First published in Great Britain 2012
by Mills & Boon, an imprint of Harlequin (UK) Limited.
Harlequin (UK) Limited, Eton House, 18-24 Paradise Road,
Richmond, Surrey TW9 1SR

© Maisey Yates 2012

ISBN: 978 0 263 89120 1

Printed and bound in Spain
by Blackprint CPI, Barcelona

A GAME OF VOWS

CHAPTER ONE

HANNAH WESTON swore as she tripped over the hem of her wedding dress, her focus diverted by the scrolling numbers on the screen of her smart phone. She'd said she wouldn't work today. She'd lied.

The exchange was closed today, but she had a lead and she needed to chase it up before she made her vows. She had clients depending on her. And he would never know.

She dropped into the limo, her eyes still trained on her phone as she gathered her dress up into a satin ball and pulled it inside, slamming the door behind her.

"Going to the chapel?"

Hannah froze, her blood turning to ice as the limo pulled away from the curb and headed into the San Francisco traffic. That voice. She knew that voice.

She couldn't look up, her eyes still set on her phone. She curled her fingers more tightly around the heavy fabric of her wedding gown, as she took a breath and raised her gaze, locking with the dark, intense eyes in the rearview mirror.

She knew those eyes, too. No one had eyes like him. They seemed to cut through you, possessing the ability to read your innermost secrets. Able to mock and flirt in a single glance. She still saw those eyes in her dreams. And sometimes her nightmares.

Eduardo Vega. One of the many skeletons in her closet. Except, he wasn't staying put.

"And I'm going to get married," she said tightly. She didn't get intimidated. She did the intimidating. Back in NY she'd had more guts than any man on the trading room floor. She'd had Wall Street by the balls. And now, she was a force to be reckoned with in the world of finance. She didn't do fear.

"Oh, I don't think so, Hannah. Not today. Unless you're interested in getting arrested for bigamy."

She sucked in a sharp breath. "I am not a bigamist."

"You aren't single."

"Yes, I am. The paperwork was…"

"Never filed. If you don't believe me, do some research on the matter."

Her stomach squeezed tight, the world tilting to the side. "What did you do, Eduardo?" His name tasted so strange on her tongue. But then, it had never been familiar. He was a stranger, essentially, her ex-husband. She had never known him, not really.

They had lived together, sort of. She'd inhabited the spare room in his luxury penthouse for six months. They hadn't shared meals, except on weekends when they'd gone to his parents' home. They hadn't shared a bed. Hadn't shared more than the odd hello when they were in his massive home. It was only in public that he'd ever really talked to her. That he'd ever touched her.

He had been quick, blessed with money, a strategic mind and a total lack of caring in regards to propriety. She'd never met a man like him. Before or since. Of course, she hadn't been blackmailed into marriage before or since, either.

"Me?" His eyes met hers in the mirror again, a smile curving his lips, a flash of white teeth against dark skin. "Nothing."

She laughed. "That's funny. I don't believe you. I signed the papers. I remember it very clearly."

"And you might have known they were never finalized if you had left a forwarding address for your mail. But that's not the way you do things, is it? Tell me, are you still running, Hannah?"

"What did you do?" she asked, refusing to let his last barb stick in its target. She didn't have to answer to Eduardo. She didn't have to answer to anyone. And she most definitely didn't have to run.

She met his eyes in the mirror and felt a sharp pang of emotion that mocked her previous thought. Why was this happening now? She was getting married in an hour. To Zack Parsons, the best man she'd ever known. He was respectful, and honorable. Distant. Able to help give her a career boost. He was everything she wanted, everything she needed.

"It's a complicated process," he said, his accent as charming as ever, even as his words made her blood boil. "Something perhaps...went amiss?"

"You bastard! You utter bastard!" She shut the web browser on her phone and pulled up the number pad, poised to dial.

"What are you doing, Hannah?"

"Calling...the police. The national guard."

"Your fiancé?"

Her stomach tightened down on itself. "No. Zack doesn't need to know...."

"You mean you didn't tell your lover about your husband? Not a great foundation for a marriage."

She couldn't call Zack. She couldn't let Eduardo anywhere near the wedding. It would topple everything she'd spent the past nine years building. She hated that he had the power to do that. Hated facing the truth that he'd had power over her from the moment she'd met him.

She gritted her teeth. "Neither is blackmail."

"We traded, *mi tesoro*. And you know it. Blackmail makes it sound sordid."

"It was. It continues to be."

"And your past is so clean you can't stand getting your hands dirty? We both know that's not true."

A very rude word hovered on the edge of her lips. But freaking out at Eduardo wasn't going to solve her problem. The very pressing problem that she needed to get to the hotel and take vows. "I'm going to ask you again, before I open the door and roll out into midday traffic and completely destroy this gown: What do you want? How do I give it to you? Will it make you go away?"

He shook his head. "I'm afraid not. I'm taking you back to my hotel. And I'm not going away."

Her lip curled. "Have you got a thing for women in wedding dresses? Because you got me into one quickly last time we met, and now you seem interested in me again...and here I am in a wedding dress."

"It's not the dress."

"Give me one good reason not to call the police and tell them I've been kidnapped."

"Hannah Mae Hackett."

Her real name sounded so unfamiliar now. Even more so coming from him instead of being spoken with a Southern twang. Even still, a lead weight settled in her stomach when he said it.

"Don't even say it," she bit out.

"You don't like your name? Well, I imagine not. You *did* change it."

"Legally. I am *legally* not that name anymore. My name is Hannah Weston now."

"And you *illegally* gained scholarships, and entrance, to the university in Barcelona by falsifying your school records."

She clenched her teeth, her pulse pounding hard. She was so very screwed. And he knew it. "This sounds like a conversation we had five years ago. If you recall, I already married you to keep you from spreading it around."

"Unfinished business."

"The only thing unfinished, apparently, is our divorce."

"Oh, no, there is so much more than that." He pulled the

limo against a curb in front of one of the famous boutique hotels in San Francisco. Marble, gold trimming and sharply dressed valets signaled the luxury of the place to everyone in the area. It was the sort of thing that had drawn her from the time she was young. The sort of thing she'd really started hungering for when she realized she had the power to change her circumstances.

Every time she checked into a hotel, as soon as the door was closed and she was isolated from the world, she would twirl in a circle and fall onto the bed, reveling in the softness. The cleanliness. The space and solitude. Even now that she had her own penthouse with thousand thread count sheets, she still did it.

The hotel wasn't evoking those kinds of feelings in her today. Not with Eduardo present.

The valet took the keys and Eduardo came to Hannah's door, opening it. "Wait…did you steal this?" she asked, looking at the limo.

As Eduardo bent down, Hannah fought the urge to shrink back. "I bought it from the chauffeur. Told him to go buy one that was newer. Nicer."

"And he didn't seem to care that he was supposed to pick me up?"

"Not when I gave him enough money for two new limousines. No."

"He was going to leave a bride stranded on her wedding day?"

Eduardo shrugged. "The world is filled with dishonest and self-serving people. You, my dear, should know all about that."

She snorted and rucked her dress up over her knees, climbing out of the car without touching Eduardo. She straightened and let her dress fall neatly into place. Then she tugged on her veil, fanning it over her shoulders. "Don't say it like you aren't one of the self-serving, my darling husband."

She looked at him fully. He was still everything he'd been five years ago. Tall, broad, arresting, a vision of perfect male beauty in his well-cut suit. His bronzed skin was highlighted perfectly by his white dress shirt; his dark hair reached the collar of his jacket.

He'd always made her feel like someone had put both hands on her shoulders and shaken her. He'd always had the power to disrupt the order of her life, to make her feel like she was dangerously close to losing the control she'd worked so hard to cultivate over the years.

It was the thing she'd always hated most about him. That he was so darned magnetic. That he always had the power to make her tremble when nothing else could.

It wasn't just that he was good-looking. There were a lot of good-looking men in the world, and she was too much in control of herself to let that affect her. It was the fact that he exuded a kind of power that she could never hope to achieve. And that he had power over her.

She breezed past him, ignoring the scent of his cologne and skin, ignoring the way it made her stomach tighten. She strode into the hotel lobby, well aware that she was making a spectacle and not caring at all. She breathed in deep. She needed focus. She needed to find out what he wanted so she could leave, as quickly as possible.

"Mrs. Vega, Mr. Vega." A woman that Hannah assumed was a manager, rounded the check-in desk with a wide, money-motivated grin on her face. "So lovely to have you here. Mr. Vega told me he would be bringing his bride when he came to stay this time. So romantic."

She had to bite back a tart curse.

Eduardo closed the distance between them and curled his arm around her waist. Her breath rushed from her body. For a moment, just one crazy moment, she wanted to lean against him. To draw closer to his masculine strength. But only for a moment.

"Very," he said.

"Is there liquor in the room?" she asked, wiggling away from him.

The manager, whose name tag identified her as Maria, frowned slightly. "There is champagne waiting for you."

"We'll need three," she said.

Maria's frown deepened. "I…"

"She's kidding," Eduardo said.

Hannah shook her head. "I've been hammered since I took my vows. I intend to spend the rest of the day that way."

"We'll just go upstairs."

"Send champagne," Hannah said as Eduardo attempted to drag her from the desk in what she imagined he thought was a loving, husbandly manner.

He ushered her into a gilded elevator, a smile pasted on his darkly handsome face until the door closed behind them.

"That was not cute, Hannah," he said.

She put her hand on her hip and gave him her sassiest smile. She didn't feel sassy, or in control, but she could fake it with the best of them. "Are you kidding me? I think I'm ready for my close-up. That was fine acting."

He shot her a bland look. "Your entire life has been acting. Don't expect accolades now."

Her smile faltered for a moment. "Look, I am on edge here."

"You aren't crying. No gnashing of teeth over leaving your fiancé at the altar."

She bit the inside of her cheek. "You don't know anything about my relationship with Zack, so don't pretend you do. I care about him. I don't want to leave him at the altar. I want you to come to your senses and give me the keys to your ill-gotten limo so I can drive myself to the hotel and marry him." The image of Zack, in that black, custom tux, standing in front of all of their friends and coworkers…it made her feel sick. She'd never, ever intended to put him through that kind of humiliation. The idea of it being reversed made her skin crawl.

"Whether I drive you there or not, your marriage won't be legal. I explained that already."

"They gave me a marriage license," she said, her voice sounding distant, echoey. Her hands were starting to shake. Why was she reacting this way? Why was she being so weak? Was she in shock?

"And we were married, and attempted to divorce out of your home country. Things get missed."

"How could something this important just get missed?" she said, exploding. "I don't believe for one second you… *forgot* to file the papers."

His smile turned dark. "Stranger things have happened, *tesoro*."

For the first time she noticed that he wasn't exactly the same. She'd thought his eyes the same, but she saw now they weren't. He used to sparkle. His brown eyes glittering with mischief. He'd been so amused at finding out her secret, that she wasn't who she'd claimed to be. He'd been even more amused at the thought of marrying an American girl to gall his father, when he'd mandated his son take a wife to gain leadership of their company. To prove he was a family man. It had been the best joke to him, to marry a college student with no money, no connections and no cooking skills.

The sparkle was gone now. Replaced with a kind of black glitter that seemed to suck the light from the room, that seemed to absorb any kind of brightness and kill it. It did something strange to her. Pulled at her like the sparkle never had.

"Like getting kidnapped on your wedding day?"

"Coerced away, perhaps. But don't tell me you haven't got pepper spray somewhere in your purse. You could have stopped me. You could have called the police. You could have called your Zack. You didn't. And you still aren't doing it.

You could turn and walk out of this room right now and get a cab. I wouldn't stop you. And you know that."

"But you *know*. You know everything. And I…"

"And it would ruin your reputation with your clients. No one wants to hear their financial adviser is a high school dropout who committed fraud to get her college degree."

"You're right, that kind of information does make client meetings awkward," she said, her voice flat, a sick feeling settling in her stomach.

"I imagine so. Just remember how awkward it made our meeting back when you were my intern."

"I think the real awkwardness came when you blackmailed me into marrying you."

"You keep using that word. Was it really blackmail?"

"According to Webster's Dictionary? Yes."

He shrugged. "Either way, had you not had something for me to hold over your head…it wouldn't have worked."

"You're so smug about it," she said, seething now. The clock on the nightstand read five minutes to her wedding and she was standing in an opulent hotel suite, in her wedding gown, with another man. "But you've had everything handed to you in your life, Eduardo. You work because your daddy gave you an office. I had to make my own destiny, and maybe…maybe the way I went about it was a little bit shady."

"The United States government calls it fraud. But *shady* is fine."

"You have no idea what it's like," she said.

"No, you're right. I can hardly speak around the silver spoon in my mouth. What would I know about hardship?" His lip curled, his expression hard, cynical. A new look for Eduardo.

"Your only hardship was that your father demanded you give up your life as a partying man whore and find a wife. So what did you do? You twisted my arm, because you thought a *gringa* wife, especially one who wasn't Catholic and couldn't cook, would be a funny way to follow your father's orders without actually following them. And I went along with it, because it was better than losing my job. Better than getting kicked out of university. Everything was a game to you, but to me, it was life."

"You're acting like I hurt you in some way, Hannah, but we both know that isn't true. I gave you your own room. Your own wing of the penthouse. I never intruded on you, never once took advantage of you. I kept to our agreement and released you from our bargain after six months, and you left. With all the money I promised you," he said. "You keep forgetting the money I gave you."

She clenched her teeth. "Because I didn't spend it." She hadn't been able to. Leaving him, or more to the point, his family and the city that had started to feel like home, had felt too awful. And she'd felt, for the first time, every inch the dishonorable person she was. "If you want your ten thousand dollars, it's in a bank account. And frankly, it's pennies as far as I'm concerned at this point."

"Oh, yes, you are very successful now, aren't you?"

She didn't feel it at the moment. "Yes. I am."

Eduardo advanced toward her. "You are good with finances, investments."

"Financial planning, strategies, picking stocks. You name it, I'm good at it."

"That's what I want from you."

"What? Financial advice?"

"Not exactly." He looked out the window, his expression inscrutable. "My father died two years ago."

An image of the hard, formidable, amazing man that Eduardo had been blessed enough to call his father swam before her eyes. Miguel Vega had been demanding. A taskmaster. A leader. He had cared. About his business, about his children. About his oldest son, who wasn't taking life seriously enough. Cared enough to back him into a corner and force him to marry. It was a heavy-handed version of caring, but it was more than Hannah had ever gotten from her own father.

Eventually, that man, his wife, Eduardo's sister, had come to mean something to her. She'd loved them.

"I'm so sorry," she said, her voice muted now, a strange kind of grief filling her heart. Not that Miguel would have missed or cared about her. And she didn't deserve it. She'd lied to him. And as far as he was concerned, she'd left his son.

"As am I," Eduardo said. "But he left me in charge of Vega Communications."

"And things aren't going well?"

"Not exactly." A muscle in his jaw ticked. "No, not exactly."

"Do you need me to look at your books? Because I can do that after I marry Zack."

He shook his head, his dark eyes blazing. "That can't happen, *tesoro*."

"But it can," she said, desperation filling her again. It was past bridal-march time. She could just picture the hotel, all decked out in pink ribbon and tulle. Her beautiful pink wedding cake. It was her dream wedding, the dream she'd had since she was a little girl. Not some traditional wedding in a cathedral, conducted entirely in Latin. A wedding that was a show for the groom's family. A wedding that had nothing to do with her.

It was a wedding with a groom who didn't love her, but at least liked her. A groom who didn't find the idea of taking vows with her to be a joke. He at least wanted her around. Being wanted on a personal level was new for her. She liked the way it felt.

"Sorry, Hannah. I need you to come back to Spain with me." He looked out the window. "It's time I brought my wife back home."

"No is the same in both of our languages, so there should

be nothing lost in translation when I say no." Hannah took a step back; her calf connected with the soft edge of the mattress, her dress rustling with the motion.

"Sorry, but this isn't a negotiation. Either you come with me now, or I march you down the aisle at the hotel myself, and you can explain, in front of your guests, and your groom, exactly why you can't marry him today. How you were about to involve him in an illegal marriage."

"Not on purpose! I would never have done this to him if I would have known."

"Once the extent of your past history is revealed, he may not believe you. Or, even if he did, he may not want you." His lips curved up into a smile, his eyes absent of any humor. And that was when she had the very stark, frightening impression that she was looking at a stranger.

He was nothing like the Eduardo she'd once known. She didn't know how she'd missed it. How it hadn't been obvious from the moment she'd seen his eyes in the rearview mirror. Yes, he had the same perfectly curved lips, the same sharply angled jaw. The same bullheaded stubbornness. But he no longer had that carefree air he'd always conducted himself with. There were lines by his eyes, bracketing his mouth. A mouth that looked like it had forgotten how to smile.

Maybe the death of his father had taken a serious toll on him. But she didn't care. She couldn't afford to care. She had to look out for herself, just as she'd been doing all of her life. No one else would. No one else ever had.

"Bastard," she spat.

"You're getting repetitive," he said dryly.

"So what? You expect me to come back to Spain and just… be your wife?"

"Not exactly. I expect you to come back and continue to act as my wife in name only while you help me fix the issues I'm having with Vega Communications."

"Why?"

"Because I don't need anyone to know there are issues. Not my competitors, I don't need them smelling blood in the water. Not my mother, she has no need to worry. My sister… I don't want to worry her, either. No one can know." There was an edge to his voice, evidence of fraying control. She could work with that. She could definitely work with that.

The pieces started falling into place in her mind. "So you think it can look like a reconciliation five years in the making. Your wife is suddenly back in Barcelona and hanging on your arm. Rather than letting anyone in on the fact that you needed to bring in outside consultation to help straighten up your finances?"

"That's the sum of it," he ground out.

It made sense now. All fine and good for him to sweep in like a marauder and demand her cooperation. But all that sweeping was hiding very real problems.

And those problems meant she had a lot more power than she'd thought she'd possessed thirty seconds earlier.

Her lips curved into a smile, the heated adrenaline she always felt when presented with a battle spreading through her chest, her limbs. "You need me. Say it."

"Hannah…"

"No. If I'm going to even consider doing this, you admit it. To me, and to yourself. You never would back then, but now…now I'm not a scared college student trying to hold on to my position at school." She met his eyes without flinching. "Admit that you need me."

"You were never a scared college student," he bit out. "You were an angry one. Angry you'd been caught out and desperate to do anything to keep it secret."

"Well, now you're sounding a little desperate." She crossed her arms beneath her breasts and cocked her hip to the side. "So, at least say please."

His lip curled into a sneer, a muscle in his jaw ticking. He was weighing his options. "Please."

She tilted her chin up and smiled, the sort of smile she knew would make his blood boil. "Good boy."

The feral light in his eyes let her know that she'd just about gone too far. She didn't care. He couldn't screw up her day any more than he already had.

He didn't move for a beat. She could see him, calculating, making decisions. For a moment she thought he might reach out and grab her. Take her in his arms and...strike her? Certainly not. No matter what Eduardo was, he wasn't a monster. Kiss her?

That he might do. The thought made her stomach tighten, made her heart beat faster.

She saw him visibly relax. "A lot of confidence and attitude coming from a woman who could face criminal charges if the right words were spoken into the wrong ears."

She put her hands on her hips. "But you showed your hand, darling," she said, turning his use of endearments back at him. "I may be over a barrel, but you're tied to me. If I go over the cliff, you're coming, too. I might be stuck, but you're just as stuck. So, let's be civil, you and I, huh?"

"Let's not forget who stands to lose the most," he said, his voice hard.

She examined his face, the hard lines etched into it. Brackets around his mouth, creases in his forehead. Lines that had appeared sometime in the past five years, for they hadn't been there back when she'd first met him. "I have a feeling you might have a bit more to lose than you're letting on."

"What about you? At the least you stand to lose clients, your reputation. At the most?"

He didn't have to finish the sentence. It was possible she could lose...so much. Everything. That she could face criminal charges. That she could find herself with her degree revoked. That she could find herself back in Arkansas in a single-wide mobile home that had a lawn with more pink plastic flamingos than it had grass.

She couldn't go back to that. To that endless, blank hell that had no end. No beginning. No defining moments. Just an eternity of uncomfortable monotony that most people she'd lived around had tried to dull with the haze of alcohol or the high of drugs.

No. She wasn't taking any chances on returning to that life. Not ever.

"Your point is taken," she said. "Anyway…I can't go and marry Zack now, no matter what, can I?"

"Not unless you want to extend your list of criminal activity."

"I didn't hurt anyone, Eduardo," she said stiffly.

Eduardo surveyed the slim, cool blonde standing in front of him, arms crossed over the ornate bodice of her wedding dress. His wife. Hannah. One of the images in his mind that had remained bright and clear, no matter how thick the fog was surrounding other details, other memories.

His vision of her as a skinny college student with a sharp mind and more guts than any person he'd ever met, had stayed with him. And when he'd realized just how much of a struggle things were becoming with Vega Communications, it had been her image he'd seen in his mind. And he'd known that he had to get his wife back.

His wife. The wife who had never truly been his wife beyond her signature on the marriage certificate. But she was a link. To his past. To the man he'd been. To those images that were splintered now, like gazing into a shattered mirror. He had wondered if seeing her could magically put him back there. If she could make the mirror whole. Reverse things, somehow.

Foolish, perhaps. But he couldn't get her out of his mind, and there had to be a reason. Had to be a reason she was so clear, when other things simply weren't.

Thankfully, he'd managed to get his timing just right. And

in his new world, one of migraines and half-remembered conversations, good timing was a rarity he savored.

"Does that make falsifying school records all right, then?" he said, watching her gray-blue eyes turn a bit more gray. A bit more stormy, as she narrowed them in his direction.

He personally didn't care what she'd done to get into university. Back then, he'd selected her to be his intern based on her impeccable performance in college, and not on anything else. Clearly she'd been up to the task, and in his mind, that was all that mattered.

But he'd use every bit of leverage he had now, and he wouldn't let his conscience prick him over it. Hannah knew all about doing what had to be done. And that's what he was doing now.

"I don't suppose it does," she said tightly. "But I don't dwell on that. I gave myself a do-over in life, and I've never once regretted it. I've never once looked back. I messed up when I was too young to understand what that might mean to my future, and when I did realize it…when it was too late…"

"You acted. Disregarding the traditional ideas of right and wrong, disregarding who it might hurt. And that's what I'm doing now. So I hope you'll forgive me," he said, aware that no sincerity was evident in his voice. He felt none.

She was testing him, needling him, trying to make him angry. It had worked, but it wouldn't divert his focus. She was his focus.

"So you think that makes it okay?" Her full lips turned down.

"I'm not overly concerned with questions of morality at the moment. I need to drag Vega back up to where it belongs."

"How is it you've managed to let it get so bad?" she said, again, not hesitating to throw her own barbs out.

There was no way in hell he was talking about his shortcomings. Not now. Maybe not ever. It wasn't her concern.

"We all have strengths," he said tightly. "It's the budget I'm having an issue with. Investments. Taxes. I am not an expert."

"Hire someone."

"I did. He didn't do his job."

"Basically, you didn't notice that he was screwing up?"

The thought of it, of trying to keep track of that, plus the day-to-day running of Vega, made his head swim, made his temples pound. His breath shortened, became harder to take in. Panic was a metallic taste on his tongue.

Would he ever feel normal? Or was this normal now? Such a disturbing thought. One he didn't have time to dwell on.

"I didn't have time," he gritted.

"Too busy sleeping around?" she asked.

"Different heiress every night," he said, almost laughing out loud at his own lie.

"Better than toying with the domestic staff, I suppose. Or blackmailing interns into marriage."

"Ours was a special case," he said.

"Oh, yes, indeed. I suppose that's why I feel suffused with a warm glow of specialness."

He chuckled, gratified when Hannah looked stymied by the reaction. She wanted to make him angry. He wouldn't allow it. One of the gifts of his head injury, one of the few. It had cooled his passions, and while that had been inconvenient in some ways, in others, it had proven valuable. He was no longer hotheaded. Usually. No longer impulsive. According to some, he was no longer fun. But he didn't know how to fix that. He found he didn't care anymore. Another gift.

"Well, it is your big day. Shouldn't a bride feel special?"

She uttered a truly foul word and sat on the edge of the bed, the white skirt of her dress billowing out around her. Like an angry, fallen, snow angel. "Low."

"Do you love this man? The one you were meant to marry today?" He found that did trouble his conscience, even if it was only a bit of trouble.

She shook her head slowly. "No."

He shook his head. "Using someone else?"

"Hardly using him. Zack doesn't love me, either. Neither of us have time for some all-consuming passionate affair. But we *like* each other. I like him. I don't like the idea of him being stood up. I don't like the idea of humiliating him."

"More humiliating, I think, if he finds out his almost-wife has been lying to him. About so many things."

She looked down at her fingernails. "Zack has his secrets. He doesn't think anyone realizes it…but he has them. I can tell. And I know better than to ask about them."

"And that means…"

"He would have accepted that I had mine. We didn't share everything."

"I doubt he intended to share you with another husband."

"Well, it's not going to happen now." A brief expression of vulnerability, sadness, crossed Hannah's features. And as quickly as he'd glimpsed it, it disappeared. Clearly, she had some amount of feeling for her lover, no matter what she said.

"Plans change." As he knew all too well.

"I have to call…someone," she said, her heart twisting.

"It's too late to salvage the day."

"I'm aware," she snapped. "Just…give me a minute."

She pulled her phone from her purse.

"Who are you calling?"

"My assistant. She's in the office minding things since I'm away. Shelby?" Her tone turned authoritative.

She paused for a moment, her cheeks turning a dull pink. "I know. I can't…I can't go through with it. It's complicated. And I can't get to the hotel." She gave him a pointed look. "Can you drive over and…and tell Zack?"

"Tell him what?" Eduardo heard her assistant's shriek from where he was standing.

"That I'm sorry. That I wish I had been brave enough to do

it differently but I can't. I know it's rush hour and it's going to take forever, but please?" Hannah paused again.

"Thank you. I…I have to go." She hit the end call button and rounded on him. "I hope you're pleased with yourself." He wasn't, not then. But this wasn't about how he felt. This was about what had to be done. This was about trying to fix Vega. Trying to fix himself.

"Not really. But I promise you in the end you will be."

"I doubt that."

"Once everything is resolved I will give you permission to speak of your part in the resurrection of my family's company."

He hadn't intended on giving her that much. The offer shocked him. He wasn't usually spontaneous anymore.

"Really?" she asked, her expression guarded, but the interest in her eyes too keen for her to conceal entirely.

"Really. I promise, in the end, I'll divorce you and you can crow your achievements. What I don't want is anyone undercutting the business while it's vulnerable. But afterward, say whatever you like, drag me through the mud, talk about my inadequacies. It's only pride," he said. Pride he'd had to give up a long time ago. He clung to what he could, but it was limited.

"You'll really divorce me this time? Forgive me for not trusting you."

"If you don't move around like a gypsy, then you should get papers letting you know when everything is final." The first aborted divorce hadn't been intentional. Another side effect of the accident that had changed everything. But, this side effect happened to be a very fortunate one indeed.

"Fine. We have a deal." Hannah extended her slender hand and he grasped it in his. She was so petite, so fine-boned. It gave the illusion of delicacy when he knew full well she possessed none. She was steel beneath that pale skin.

A smile curved his lips, satisfaction burning in his chest. "Good girl."

CHAPTER TWO

"You made me buy my own ticket." Hannah stood in the doorway of Eduardo's penthouse, exhausted and wrinkled from travel, still angry at the way everything had transpired. She'd had short notice, and limited options. She'd had to fly economy.

An infuriating smile curved Eduardo's lips. "I did. But I knew you could afford it."

"Doesn't chivalry dictate you buy your blackmailed wife's plane ticket?" Hannah dropped her suitcase next to her feet and crossed her arms. The most shocking thing about Eduardo's appearance had been his departure, with a demand that she meet him in Barcelona in twenty-four hours. And she could get there herself.

It had been a blow to her pride, and he knew it. Because she'd been forced to get herself to Spain. She'd been the one to board the plane. If he'd tied her up and thrown her into cargo she could have pretended he'd truly forced her. That she was a slave to him, rather than to the mistakes of her past and her intense need to keep them secret.

But there was nothing more important than her image. Than the success she'd earned. Than never, ever going back to that dark place she'd come from.

Because of that, she was a slave to Eduardo, and a coward where Zack was concerned. More than a day since their almost-wedding and she hadn't called him. Of course, he hadn't called her, which spoke volumes about the quality and nature of their relationship.

"I checked and there was no specific entry in the hand-book about the most chivalrous way to force one's estranged bride to come and do their bidding."

"What's the point of even having a handbook, then?" She let out a long breath and looked pointedly at the doorway Eduardo was blocking with his broad frame. "Aren't you going to invite me into our home?"

"Of course," he said.

They'd shared the penthouse for six months five years ago. They'd been the most bizarre six months of her life. Sharing a home with a man who hardly acknowledged her presence, unless he needed her for a gala or to make a show of togeth-erness at a family dinner.

It was a six months she'd done a very good job of scrub-bing from her mind. Like every other inconvenient detail in her past, it had been chucked into her mental closet, the door locked tight. It was where every juicy secret belonged. Behind closed, difficult-to-access doors.

But now it was all coming back. Her fourth year in Spain, when she'd been accepted into a coveted internship at Vega Communications. Everything had been going so well. She'd started making connections, learning how things worked at a massive corporation.

Then one day, the boss's son had called her into his office and closed the door.

Then he'd told her he'd done a little digging and found out her real name. That she wasn't Hannah Weston from Manhattan, but that she was Hannah Hackett from Arkansas. That she hadn't graduated top of her class, but that she had no diploma at all.

And then, with supreme, enraging arrogance he had leaned back in his chair; hands behind his head; humor, mocking, glittering in his eyes, and he'd told her that her secret would be safe.

If she would marry him.

That sickening, surreal moment when she'd agreed, because there was nothing in the world that could compel her to lose the ground she'd gained.

Eduardo stepped aside and she breezed past him, leaving her suitcase for him to handle. Things were rearranged. His furniture new, but still black and sleek. The appliances in his kitchen were new, too, as was the dining set.

But the view was the same. Cathedral spires rising above gray brick buildings, touching the clear sky. She'd always loved the city.

She'd hated Eduardo for forcing her into marriage. Had hated herself nearly as much for being vulnerable to him, for needing to keep her secrets so badly.

And then she'd moved into his home, and she'd started to think the forced marriage wasn't so bad after all. It was so expansive, plush, and refined. Like nothing she'd ever experienced.

Secretly, shamefully, she'd loved it. As long as she could ignore the big Spaniard that lived there, too, everything was wonderful. Comfortable.

She'd made it into school, but she was still living on a meager budget. And Eduardo had shown her luxury she'd never seen before. She'd thought she'd known. She hadn't. Her imagination hadn't even scratched the surface of what true wealth meant. Not until she'd met the Vega family.

It had given her something to aspire to.

"Everything looks…great." Surreal. She'd never gone back to a place before. When she left, she left. Her childhood home, Spain, her place in New York.

"Updated a bit. But your room is still available."

"Haven't had any other temporary wives in my absence?"

"No, unlike some people I think having more than one spouse at a time is a bit too ambitious."

"Yes, well, you know it wasn't my intention to have more than one," she bit out, a sour feeling settling in her stomach. "Zack was decent, you know." She eyed the open door, and her suitcase, still occupying their position in the hall. "He was one of the few truly good people I've ever met. I hate that I did this to him."

"Have you been in contact?"

"No."

"Perhaps you should…?"

She clenched her teeth. "I don't know if that's such a good idea. Anyway, he hasn't called me, and he didn't come by my house, so, maybe he doesn't care." That actually hurt a little.

"If he thinks you're missing, he may send out a search party. I didn't think you wanted to publicize our marriage. Or rather, why you ran out on your wedding. It doesn't matter either way to me."

She swore and took her phone from her purse. "Fine. But Shelby did go and speak to him." She bit her lip and looked down at the screen. Still no calls from him, and she'd been sort of hoping there would have at least been one. There was a text from Shelby.

"And have you heard from him?"

"No." Strange. But she couldn't really imagine Zack playing the part of desperate, jilted groom. Decent he was, but the man had pride. She opened the text from Shelby and her heart plummeted. "Zack wasn't at the hotel when she arrived."

"So he still hasn't heard from you at all."

She clutched the phone tightly against her chest. Eduardo was watching her far too closely. She needed a moment. Just a moment.

"Why don't you bring my bags in?" she asked.

Dark eyes narrowed, but he walked over to the entry and pulled her bags just inside the door, shutting it behind him.

She bit her lip and looked back down at her phone.

"Scared?" he asked.

"No," she muttered. She opened up the message screen and typed in Zack's name, her fingers hovering over the letters on the touch screen as she watched the cursor blink. She really didn't know what to say to him. "Nothing about this in the chivalry handbook?" she asked.

Eduardo crossed his arms over his broad chest and leaned against the back of the couch. "I think we both have to accept that we're on the wrong side of honor at this point in time."

"Good thing I never gave honor much thought," she said.

Except she was now. Or at least giving thought to what a mess she'd made out of Zack's life. She growled low in her chest and shot Eduardo one last evil glare.

I'm so sorry about the wedding, Zack.

She let her thumb hover over the send button and then hit it on a groan.

"What did you tell him?"

"Nothing really yet." She pulled up another text window.

I met someone else. I— She paused for a moment and looked at Eduardo. If she'd been speaking, she would have gagged on the next word. —love him.

She closed her eyes and hit Send. Let him think that emotion had been in charge. She and Zack were both so cynical about love...he might even find it funny. That had been the foundation of their relationship really. Zack had wanted a wife, the stability marriage would bring. But he wanted a wife who wouldn't bother him about his long working hours, and who didn't want children. Or love.

They'd been so well suited.

"There. I hope you're happy. I just ruined things with my best bet for a happy ending."

"You said you didn't love him," Eduardo said.

"I know. But I like him. I respect him. How often do you get that in a marriage?"

"I don't know. I've only ever had separate bedrooms and blackmail in my marriage. What excuse did you give him?"

"I told him how much I loved you, dearest," she bit out.

He chuckled. "You always were an accomplished little liar."

"Well, I don't feel good about this one."

"You felt good about the others?"

She truly didn't know the answer. "I...I never thought about how I felt about it. Just about whether or not it was necessary. Anyway, I don't lie as a matter of course."

"You just lie about really big things infrequently?"

"Every job application has started with questions about college. Didn't I get near-perfect grades at university? Didn't I have a prestigious internship at Vega Communications? No lies. No one wants to know about high school, not once you've been through university."

"And your fiancé?"

"Never asked many questions. He liked what he knew about me." And neither of them knew all that much. Something she was realizing now that she was being haunted by her past. She and Zack had never even slept together. Not for lack of attraction. She'd been quite attracted to him, impossible not to be, but until things were legal and permanent between them she'd felt the need to hang on to that bit of control.

It was so much easier to deny her sex drive than to end up back where she'd been nine years ago. Being that girl, that was unacceptable. She never would be again.

"Lies by omission are still lies, *querida*."

"Then we're all liars."

"Now, that's true enough."

"Show me to my room," she said, affecting her commanding, imperious tone. The one she had gotten so good at over the years. "I'm tired."

A slow smile curved his lips and she fought the urge to punch him.

"Of course, darling."

This time, he picked up her bags without incident and she followed him into her room. Her room. Her throat tightened. Her first experience with homecoming. Why should it mean anything? He had replaced the bedding. A new dark-colored comforter, new sable throw pillows, new satin curtains on the windows to match. The solid desk she'd loved to work at was still in its corner. Unmoved. There was no dust on it, but then, Eduardo had always had a great housekeeper.

"This is…perfect," she said.

"I'm glad you still like it. I remember you being…giddy over it back when we were first married."

"It was the nicest room I'd ever been in," she said, opting to give him some honesty, a rare thing from her. "The sheets were…heaven."

"The sheets?"

She cleared her throat. "I have a thing for high-quality sheets. And you definitely have them here."

"Well, now you get to live here again. And reap the benefits of the sheets."

She arched a brow. "My fiancé was a billionaire, you know."

"Yes, I know. I would expect you to find nothing less," he said.

"I'm not sure how I feel about your assessment of my character, Eduardo. You express no shock over Zack's financial status, or over the fact that we weren't in love."

"You're mercenary. I know it…you know it. It's not shocking."

She *was* mercenary. If being mercenary meant she did what she had to to ensure her own success. Her own survival. She'd needed to be. To move up from the life she'd been born into. To overcome the devastating consequences of her youthful actions. And she'd never lost a wink of sleep over it. But for some reason, the fact that it was so obvious to Eduardo was a little bit unsettling.

"Is it mercenary to try and improve the quality of your life?" she asked.

"It depends on the route you take."

"And the resources available to you are a major factor in deciding which route to take," she said.

"I'm not judging you, Hannah, believe it or not."

She planted her hands on her hips. "No, you're just using me."

"As you said, you do what you must to improve the quality of your life." His expression was strange, tense. Dark.

She looked away. "I have to do something."

"What is that?"

She looked down at her left hand, at the massive, sparkly engagement ring Zack had given her a few months earlier. She tugged it off her finger, a strange sensation moving through her like a strong wind. Sadness. Regret. Relief.

"I have to send this to Zack." She held it up and realized her hands were shaking. She couldn't keep it. Not for another second. Because mercenary she might be. But she wasn't a thief. She wouldn't take from Zack. Wouldn't do any more damage than she'd already done.

"I can have someone do that for you. Do you know where he is?"

"Thailand," she said, without missing a beat. "We were supposed to honeymoon there."

"And you think he went?" he asked, dark eyebrows raised.

She smiled. "Zack had business in Thailand, so yes, I think he went. No, I know he went. He's not the kind of man to let a little thing like an interrupted marriage keep him from accomplishing his goals."

Eduardo studied her, dark eyes intense. "Perhaps he was perfect for you."

"Yeah, well, I'm trying not to dwell on that." She held the ring out and Eduardo opened his hand. She dropped it into his palm. "I have the address of the place we were meant to stay at."

"*Bien.* I'll call a courier and have it rushed." He closed his hand around the ring, the glittering gem disappearing. All she could think of was that he held her future in his hand. The future that might have been. The one that was not eclipsed by Eduardo.

She looked up, their eyes clashing. Her throat tightened, halting her breath.

"Good," she said, barely able to force out the words. She turned to the desk and saw a pad and pen slotted into the wooden slats built into it for organization. It was where she'd kept them when she'd lived here. She bent and scribbled the address for the house she should be in now, with Zack.

Her fingers felt stiff and cold around the pen. She straightened and handed him the note. "There. That should do it."

"I'm surprised you don't want to keep the ring."

"Why? I didn't keep the one you gave me, either."

"We had a prior agreement. I get the feeling you didn't have an agreement like that with him."

"Separate beds, separate lives, unless a public appearance is needed? No. We were meant to be married for real." She swallowed hard. "And all things considered, I don't feel right keeping his ring. I was the one who wronged him."

"Careful, Hannah, I might start thinking you grew a conscience in our time apart."

"I've always had one," she said. "It's been inconvenient sometimes."

"Not too inconvenient."

"Oh, what would you know about a conscience, Eduardo?"

"Very little. Only that it occasionally takes the form of a cricket."

A reluctant laugh escaped her lips. "That sounds about

right. So…if you could mail my ring to him, that would be great."

"I'll call now." He turned and walked out of the room, leaving her alone.

She sat on the edge of the bed, her emotions a blank. She wasn't sure what she was supposed to feel. Why she suddenly felt more relieved than upset about leaving Zack behind. Marriage to him would have been good.

And yet, when she thought of the honeymoon, when she thought of sharing his bed…she couldn't make the man in her vision Zack.

The man she saw was darker, more intense. The man she saw was Eduardo. His hands on her skin, his lips on her throat…

She flopped backward and covered her face with her hands. "Stop it," she admonished herself. She rolled onto her side and grabbed a pillow, hugging it tightly to her chest. She hadn't done that since high school. Comforting then, even when the world was crumbling around her, and just as comforting now.

Eduardo had always been handsome. He'd always appealed to her. That was nothing new. But she'd never once been tempted to act on any kind of attraction while they'd lived together. It hadn't been part of her plan. And she didn't deviate from her plans. Plans, control, being the one in charge of her life, that was everything. The most important thing.

Not Eduardo's handsome face and sexy physique.

"Feeling all right?" Eduardo asked from the doorway.

She snapped back into a sitting position, pillow still locked tightly against her breasts. "Fine."

Eduardo couldn't hold back the smile that tugged at the corner of his lips. Hannah Weston, flopped on her bed like a teenage girl. A show of softness, a show of humanity, he hadn't expected from an ice queen like her. Like her reaction when he mentioned her fiancé. Like when she'd given back the other man's ring.

It suited him to think of Hannah as being above human emotion. It always had. He needed her. He didn't know all the reasons why, but he did. And that meant it was easier to believe that she would simply go with the option that benefited her most and feel no regret over leaving the inferior choice behind.

But that wasn't how she was behaving. And it gave him a strange twinge in his chest that seemed completely foreign.

Hannah stood up from the bed and put the pillow gingerly back in its place. She cleared her throat and straightened. She looked...soft for a moment. Different than he'd ever seen her before. She was beautiful, no question, more so now than she'd been as a too-thin college student.

She was still thin, but her angles had softened into curves, her cheekbones less sharp, her breasts small but round.

Instantly, an image of him pushing her on the bed, tugging her shirt up, filled his mind. He could take those breasts into his hands...suck her nipple between his lips, his teeth...

A rush of blood roared through his body, south of his belt. How long had it been since that had happened? Since he'd been aroused by an actual woman. In solitude, with a fantasy, he could certainly find release. But with a woman? One he had to somehow seduce and charm when he had no more seduction and charm left in him? That had been beyond him for quite some time.

"I can see that. You epitomize 'fine.'"

"I'm ready to find out what your game plan is, Vega," she said, crossing her arms beneath those small, gorgeous breasts.

"My game plan?"

"Yes. I don't like not knowing the score. I want to know exactly what you have planned and why."

"Tomorrow, I plan to take you to the office, to let you look at things and get a feel for the state of the company."

"All right. What else?"

He felt the need to goad her. To shake her icy composure. As she was shaking his. He took a step forward, extended his hand and brushed his knuckles over her cheek. Her skin was like a rose petal, soft and delicate. "Well, tonight, my darling bride, we dine out." Her eyes darkened, blush-pink lips parting. She was not unaffected by him. His body celebrated the victory even as his mind reminded him that this had no place in their arrangement. "I intend to show all of Barcelona that Señora Vega has returned to her husband."

CHAPTER THREE

GLAMOROUS events and upscale restaurants had become typical in Hannah's world over the past five years. But going with Eduardo wasn't.

The car ride to La Playa had been awkward. She'd dressed impeccably for the evening, as she always did, her blond hair twisted into a bun, her lips and dress a deep berry color, perfect for her complexion.

Eduardo was perfectly pressed as always in a dark suit he'd left unbuttoned and a white shirt with an unfastened collar.

All of that was as it should be. The thing that bothered her was the tension between them. It wasn't just anger, and heaven knew she should feel a whole lot of anger, but there was something else. Something darker and infinitely more powerful.

Something that had changed. It was directly linked to the change in Eduardo, the dark, enticing intensity that lived in him now. The thing she couldn't define.

The thing that made her shake inside.

Eduardo maneuvered the car up the curb and killed the engine. She opened the door and was out and halfway around the car when she nearly ran into him. Her heart stalled, her breath rushing out of her.

"I would have opened your door for you," he said.

She inhaled sharply, trying to collect herself. "And I didn't need you to."

"You're my wife, *querida,* here to reconcile with me. Don't you think I would show you some chivalry?"

"Again with the chivalry. I thought you and I established that honor wasn't our strong point."

"But it will be as far as the press is concerned. Or, more to the point, our relationship needs to seem like a strength." He leaned forward and brushed his knuckles gently over her cheekbone, just as he'd done back in the penthouse.

And just as it had done back at the penthouse, her blood pressure spiked, her heartbeat raging out of control.

She'd had a connection with Zack, and certainly physical attraction. They hadn't slept together, but they'd kissed. Quite a bit. Enough to know that they had chemistry. Now the idea of what she'd shared with Zack being chemistry seemed like a joke.

It had been easy to kiss Zack and say good-night. To walk away. His lips on hers only made her lips burn.

A look from Eduardo made her burn. Everywhere.

She'd lived with him before, though, and nothing had happened between them. There was no reason to think she couldn't keep a handle on it this time.

She turned her face away from him, the night air hitting her cheek, feeling especially cold with the loss of his skin against hers.

He cupped her chin with his thumb and forefinger, turning her face so that she had to look at him. "You can't act like my touch offends you."

"I'm not," she said, holding her breath as she took a step closer to him, as she slid her hand down his arm and laced her fingers with his. "See?"

She was sure he could hear her heart pounding, was certain he knew just how he was affecting her. Except...he wasn't gloating. He wasn't poised to give her a witty comeback, or make fun of her.

"You seem so different," she said, following him to where

the valet was standing. He ignored her statement and gave his keys to the young man in the black vest, speaking to him in Spanish, his focus determinedly off Hannah, even while he held on to her hand.

He tightened his grip on her as they walked on the cobblestones, to the front of the restaurant. It was an old building, brick, the exterior showing the age and character of Barcelona. But inside, it had been transformed. Sleek, sophisticated and smelling nearly as strongly of money as it did of paella, it was exactly the kind of place she'd imagined Eduardo would like.

It was exactly the kind of place *she* liked.

A man dressed all in black was waiting at the front. His face lit with recognition when Eduardo walked in. "Señor Vega, a table for you and your guest?"

"Sí," he said. "This is Señora Vega, my wife. She's come back to Barcelona. I'm very…pleased to see her." He turned to the side, brushing her hair off her face. Heat sparked, from there down through her body. She tried to keep smiling.

The man cocked his head to the side, clearly pleased to be let in on such exclusive news. *"Bienvenido a Barcelona, señora.* We're glad to have you back."

She could feel Eduardo's gaze on her, feel his hold tighten on her waist. She forced her smile wider. "I'm very glad to be back."

"Bien. Right this way."

He led them to a table in the back of the room, white and glossy, with bright red bench seats on either side of it. There was a stark white curtain shielding part of the seating area from view, giving an air of seclusion and luxury.

Eduardo spoke to their host in Spanish for a moment before the other man left and Eduardo swept the curtain aside, holding it open for her. She looked at him, the smile still glued on her face. "Thank you."

Back when they'd been married, they might have gone to a

place like this late on a Saturday night. And everyone inside would know Eduardo. Would clamor for his attention. And she would play her part, smiling and nodding while mentally trying to decide what appetizer to get.

There was none of that tonight. If people had looked at them, it had been subtle. And no one spoke to Eduardo. No one stopped to ask about business. Or where the next big party was. Or which nightclub was opening soon.

She looked behind them and saw that people were staring. Trying to be covert, but not doing a good job. Their expressions weren't welcoming. They looked... They looked either afraid or like they were looking at a car crash and she couldn't figure out why.

"You play your part very well," Eduardo said, not paying any attention to the other diners, "but then, you always did."

"I know," she said. She played every part well. A girl from the Southern United States with bad grades, a thick-as-molasses accent and a total lack of sophistication had to work hard to fit in with the university crowd in Barcelona. But she'd done it.

She'd dropped most of her accent, studied twice as hard as anyone else, and perfected an expression of boredom that carried her through posh events and busy cities without ever looking like the country mouse she was.

It was only when she was alone that she gave herself freedom to luxuriate in comfortable sheets and room service, and all of the other things her new life had opened up to her.

"And you're never modest, which, I confess, I quite like," he said. "Why should you be? You've achieved a great a deal. And you've done it on your own."

"Is this the part where you try and make friends with me?" she asked.

He laughed, a sort of strained, forced sound, nothing like the laugh he'd once had. It had been joyous, easy. Now he sounded out of practice. "Don't be silly, why would I do that?"

"No reason, I suppose. You never did try to be my friend. Just my fake husband."

"Your real husband," he corrected. "Ours just hasn't been a traditional marriage."

"Uh, no. Starting with you calling me into your office one day and telling me you knew all my secrets and that, unless I wanted them spilled, I would do just as you asked me."

A waiter came by and Eduardo ordered a *pre fixe* meal. Hannah read the description in the gilded menu and her stomach cramped with hunger. She was thin—she always had been—but it had more to do with her metabolism than watching her diet. Food was very important to her.

When the waiter had gone, she studied Eduardo's face again. "Why did you do that? Why did you think it would be so…funny to marry me?"

He shook his head. "Very hard to say at this point in time. Everything was a joke to me. And I felt manipulated. I resented my father's heavy hand in my life and I thought I would play his game against him."

"And you used me."

He met her eyes, unflinching. "I did."

"Why?"

He looked down, a strange expression on his face. "Because I could. Because I was Eduardo Vega. Everything, and everyone, in my life existed to please me. My father wanted to see me be a man. He wanted to see me assume control. Find a wife, a family to care for. To give of myself instead of just take. I thought him a foolish, backward old man."

"So you married someone you knew he would find unsuitable."

"I did." He looked up at her. "I would not do so now."

She studied him more closely, the hardened lines on his face, the weariness in his eyes. "You seem different," she said, finally voicing it.

"How so?" he asked.

"Older."

"I am older."

"But more than five years older," she said, looking at the lines around his mouth. Mostly though, it was the endless darkness in his eyes.

"You flatter me."

"You know I would never flatter you, Eduardo. I would never flatter anyone."

A strange expression crossed his face. "No, you wouldn't. But I suppose, ironically, that proves you an honest person in your way."

"I suppose." She looked down at the table. "Has your father's death been hard on you?"

"Of course. And for my mother it has been…nearly unendurable. She has loved him, only him, since she was a teenager. She's heartbroken."

Hannah frowned, picturing Carmela Vega. She had been such a sweet, solid presence. She'd invited Eduardo and Hannah to dinner every Sunday night during their marriage. She'd forced Hannah to know them. To love them.

More people that Hannah had hurt in order to protect herself.

"I'm very sorry about that."

"As am I." He hesitated a moment. "I am doing my best to take care of things. To take care of her. There is something you should know. Something you *will* know if you're going to spend any amount of time around me."

Anticipation, trepidation, crept over her. He sounded grave, intense, two things Eduardo had never been when she'd known him. "And that is?" she asked, trying to keep her tone casual.

Eduardo wished the waiter had poured them wine. He would have a word with the manager about the server after their meal.

Before he could answer Hannah's question, their waiter

appeared, with wine and mussels in clarified butter. He set them on the table and Eduardo picked up the glass, taking a long drink.

When the waiter left again, he set it on the table, his focus back on Hannah, his resolve strengthened.

"I was involved in an accident, very soon after you left."

"An accident?"

"At my family's stables. I was jumping my horse in a course I had ridden hundreds of times. The horse came to a jump he'd done before, but he balked. I was thrown." That much, he had been told by others later. It was strange how vividly he remembered the moments leading up to the accident. The smell of the dirt, grass and the sweat of the horses. He could remember mounting his horse and coaxing him into a trot, then a canter. He could remember nothing after that. Nothing for days and days after. They were gone. "I wasn't wearing a helmet. My head hit the edge of the jump, then the ground." The regret of that burned in him still. It had been a simple thing, a commonplace activity, and it had changed his life forever. "It's funny, because you see, I did forget to file the divorce papers."

Hannah looked pale, her cheeks the color of wax, her lips holding barely a blush of rose. For the first time since he'd known her, she looked truly shaken. "It doesn't sound funny."

"You can laugh at it, *querida*. I don't mind."

"I do. I mind, Eduardo. How badly were you hurt?"

He shook his head. "Badly enough. There has been…damage." He hated to speak of it. Hated to voice the lasting problems the accident had caused. It made them seem real. Final. He didn't want them. Five years later and he couldn't believe he was trapped with a mind that betrayed him as his did.

"I have issues with my memory," he said. "My attention span. Frequent migraines. And I have had some changes in my personality. At least I've been told so. It's hard for me to truly…remember or understand the man I was before."

He looked at her face, stricken, pained. Strange to see her that way. She had always been as cool and steady as a block of ice. Even when he'd called her into his office all those years ago to tell her he'd discovered she'd faked her paperwork to get into college, she'd been stoic. Angry, but poised.

With a calm that women twice her age couldn't have affected, she'd agreed to his foolish marriage scheme. It seemed foolish to him now, anyway. He'd been such a stupid boy, full of his own importance, laughing at life.

Yes, he certainly had changed.

Even now, sitting across from Hannah, as he had done that day he'd coerced her into marriage, he couldn't understand the man that he'd been. Couldn't understand why it had been so amusing. Why he had felt entitled to drag her into his game.

He had been convinced that being near her would…

"I noticed," she said, her voice soft.

"I suppose you did." He lifted his wineglass to his lips again, trying to ignore the defeat that came when the crisp flavor hit his tongue. Wine didn't even make him feel the same. It used to make him feel lighter, a bit happier. Now it just made him tired. "It is of no consequence. With the changes came no desire for me to change back." It wasn't true, not entirely, but he was hardly going to give her reason to pity him. He could take a great many things, but not pity.

"Is this why you're having problems with Vega?" she asked.

"Essentially." The word burned. "I had someone hired to…" He chose his words carefully. He disliked the word *help* almost as much as he disliked saying he couldn't do something. Of course, the verbal avoidance game was empty, because it didn't change reality. "To oversee the duties of managing finances and budgets. Someone else to do taxes. Neither did an adequate job, and now I find myself with some issues to work out, and no one that I trust to handle it."

"And you trust me?" Her tone was incredulous, blue eyes round.

"I don't know that I trust you, but I do know your deepest and darkest secrets. In the absence of trust, I consider it a fairly hefty insurance policy."

She took another sip of her wine. "There are some things about you that are still the same," she said.

"What things?" he asked, desperate to know.

For a moment, she felt like the lifeline he'd built her up to be. No one else seemed to see anything in him from before. They saw him as either diminished in some way, or frightening. His mother and sister, loving as ever, seemed to pity him. He felt smothered in it.

"You're still incredibly amused by what you perceive to be your own brilliance."

Unbidden, a laugh escaped his lips. "If a man can't find amusement with himself, life could become boring."

"A double entendre?" She arched her brow.

"No, I'm afraid not. Further evidence of the changes in me, I suppose." And yet with Hannah, sometimes he felt normal. Something akin to what and who he had been. It felt good to exchange banter, to have her face him, an almost-friendly adversary. For the moment.

"You're also still a stubborn, arrogant autocrat." She seemed almost determined to prove to herself that he was the same.

"As ever."

"And your father's business? Vega Communications? Is it all still a joke to you?"

"Is that what you thought? That it was a joke to me?"

She looked down. "You taking me as a wife was certainly a joke. A joke you used to convince him to pass Vega into your hands then."

"Evidence that nothing about Vega Communications was ever a joke to me."

"Because providing mobile phone service to an ever-increasing number of countries is your passion?"

"Because it's my birthright. It's part of my family legacy." And because if he failed at that, he had nothing to strive for. "Like you, I did very well at university. I earned a degree... I earned my position. Yes, I had connections, but you managed to get into Vega as an intern. You've managed to make your own connections. Why be disdainful simply because my course was more set than yours?"

She looked thoughtful as she took a mussel on the half shell between her thumb and forefinger. "I was disdainful because I never thought you cared about it. Or even wanted it. Not really."

"I expected it. I suppose, given that it seemed a certainty, I lacked the blatant desperation you possessed."

She put the mussel between her lips and sucked out the flesh. It wasn't a sexy action. Not really. And yet, when she did it, it was oddly compelling. It was because her lips managed to look sensual, inviting and soft, all while her eyes told him she'd happily bite his tongue if he dared follow the impulse that originated south of his belt.

"Desperation?" she asked, taking the white linen napkin from her lap and dabbing the side of her mouth. "Drive, maybe."

"If it makes you feel better."

"It does. Humor me."

He inclined his head. "If you wish. Anyway, I may sympathize with you a bit more now. I have to fix this. Vega is my family. My life."

The glee she'd seemed to take from her initial thought of his being desperate had diminished. "You used to like other things better."

"I did."

"Parties. Loose women."

"I was faithful to you during our marriage." A statement

more true than she realized. But the fallout from the head in-jury had been extensive. He'd lost his passion for everything. Had lost friends. He'd had a hunger for life once. For fun and pleasure, for laughter.

He had nothing more than a white-knuckled grip on exis-tence now. A human, biological need to keep breathing. And with that, came the need to save Vega.

It gave him a reason to go on, anyway, and that was, at this point in his life, more valuable than passion.

"Prince Charming in the flesh," she said lightly.

The waiter returned and set a fish course before them, Spanish rice and spiced greens on the side. Hannah wasted no time in helping herself. She had always liked eating. He'd been fascinated by it. When they would go to his family's house for dinner, she'd always eaten as much as he did, if not more. Still, she'd always looked thin. Hungry. But he'd sus-pected, even then, that her hunger wasn't for food.

She'd been hungry for money. Status. Success.

She still was. It was why she was here with him. Why he'd been able to demand she return to Spain.

"Not entirely," he said, his tone heavier than he intended it to be.

"So tell me then," she said, blue eyes glittering with mis-chief. "Will you be faithful to me during our reconciliation?" Her lips closed around her fork and his gut tightened.

"That all depends, Hannah," he said, words forming be-fore thought, his body leading the proceedings.

"On?"

"On whether or not you intend to share my bed this time."

Hannah nearly choked on her rice. "What?"

Eduardo leaned back in his chair, a dark glint in his eye, a lean, hungry look to his features. "You heard me, *querida*. Will I need to seek my amusement elsewhere? Or will you share my bed?"

"I am not sleeping with you," she said, the very idea of the invasion, the intimacy, the loss of utter and complete control, making her feel shivery and panicky. Hot.

"Then I suppose the answer to the question is not your concern."

"No," she bit out.

She didn't truly care who he slept with. She'd been trying to goad him, nothing else. They did that. They always had. Verbal sparring had been the only level they'd ever truly connected on.

They shared a love of arguing, which, in some ways, made them the perfect married couple for the public. For all she knew of married couples.

"At least we're on the same page," he said, returning his focus to his dinner.

What did that mean? That he didn't want her? That made her…mad. And it shouldn't. She shouldn't care. Men, attraction, sex, none of it fit into her life. She'd been about to make room for Zack, and of course she'd intended to sleep with him eventually. But she'd been in control of it, no question. She'd been able to wait, and so had he. She and Zack were both all about control, about keeping things in order, in their neat little boxes.

Eduardo would never fit into a box. She would never be able to shove him to one side of her life and ignore him unless she wanted to open him up and indulge. Nope. That wasn't possible. He was too much. Too…present. He was impossible to simply ignore.

She didn't want to sleep with him anyway. She'd denied her sex drive, rightly, necessarily, for the past nine years. Sure, she'd been about to end the dry spell with marriage. But it hadn't been the attractor to marrying Zack. It had never been that important. It wasn't all-consuming.

It wouldn't be with Eduardo, either. She could keep on ignoring it, no question. And Eduardo wouldn't change that.

So his lack of desire for her shouldn't matter. Her ego was just feeling bruised.

"Good thing. So," she said, "what's your plan for tomorrow? Just waltzing into the office and announcing we're reconciling?"

A smile curved his lips. An unsettling, dark smile that made her stomach tighten and her heart pound. "Why don't we just see what happens?"

CHAPTER FOUR

WHY don't we just see what happens?

Even getting out of the car the next morning, business armor in the form of a sleek-fitting pair of slacks and a dark blue button-up shirt, she heard his words playing through her head. They'd sounded like a double entendre. Like he'd disregarded the previous portion of the conversation where she'd said she wouldn't sleep with him.

Smug-ass Spaniard.

She tightened her hold on her laptop bag and chanced a glance at him out of the corner of her eye. He was looking sexier than he ever had, at least to her, in a navy suit, his dark hair left slightly disheveled, as if theirs was a reconciliation made in the bedroom.

He paused in front of the heavy glass door of the tall, modern building and held it open for her, his dark eyes never leaving hers.

She made eye contact as she walked in. She wasn't about to let him intimidate her. Nope. Not going to happen.

Her gaze was steely. She was sure of it. And his was... amused. It was the first time she'd seen him amused, really amused, in a way that reminded her of the old Eduardo, since he'd hijacked a limo and disrupted her wedding.

A leaden weight dropped into her stomach. A sudden reminder of why he'd changed.

She tossed her hair and continued into the building. She

knew it well. She'd interned there for months and then she'd become the boss's daughter-in-law. She'd learned about the way a big business ran here, had faced down Eduardo for the first time.

Another strange wave of homecoming melancholy washed over her. She tried to clear her tightened throat.

"*Buenos días,* Paola." Eduardo greeted the woman sitting behind the reception desk.

"*Buenos días, Señor Vega.*" She looked up for the first time, her eyes rounding when she saw Hannah. "Hannah," she said.

Hannah's heart beat against her breastbone. She remembered her? She'd never wondered much if people remembered her. She'd never been back to a place to find out.

"Hi, Paola." She'd always like Paola. The other woman had always been nice to her, not laughing at her mangled Spanish, always offering her a smile when she'd come in for work after classes.

She wondered what Paola had thought when she'd suddenly "abandoned" Eduardo and their six-month union.

"You're…back?" she asked, her focus darting from Eduardo and back to Hannah.

"Yes," Eduardo said, turning to her, his expression soft, the hard glint in his eye telling her the expression was a lie. "She is." He lifted his hand and brushed his finger lightly over her cheek.

A shiver wound through her, tightening her stomach, her lungs, her nipples. She'd tried to forget this part of being near him. Had tried, and failed, so many times to forget what it had felt like on their wedding day when his lips had touched hers.

To forget that he brought out a beast in her. One that was normally asleep, or at least dormant, kept mollified by the occasional fantasy and gratuitous amounts of cop shows with men in tight uniforms.

This was different than those contained, allowed moments

of desire. This was different even than the attraction she'd felt for him back when they'd first married. This wasn't something she had a grasp on; it was nothing she could control or shut off.

The wedding kiss, and feelings it had created in her, had lingered. But she'd been able to keep it where it belonged. Stored for her convenient use late at night, never invading her body or thoughts during the day. Never when it wasn't appropriate.

It was invading now.

She swallowed hard and worked at composing her face. She wasn't going to break; she wasn't going to show nerves. Or arousal. "That's right," she said. "I am."

Then, just to prove to him that he wasn't the only one who could play the game, she leaned in, pausing for a moment as his scent hit her. Sandalwood and skin. She couldn't remember ever noticing the way he smelled before. It was foreign. Sexy. Piquing her curiosity, her need to draw closer.

So she did, because that had been her intent. Not for any other reason. Her eyes met his as her lips connected with his cheek. Smooth still, clean, a hint of aftershave lingering. She closed her eyes, just for a moment, and let the feel of him beneath her lips fully wash over.

Then she pulled back, quickly, her head swimming, her heart pounding.

"Yes, I'm back," she said, blowing out a breath and smiling at Paola, trying to ignore the intense quivering in her stomach.

"Good," she said. "Very good. We're glad to have you."

"As am I," Eduardo said, his eyes never leaving Hannah. "Come, *querida,* I want to show you some of the changes I've made."

She offered Paola another smile and a stilted nod before following Eduardo into the first elevator on the right. She let out a breath when the platinum doors closed.

"Very convincing," Eduardo said, a strange smile curving his lips. It was almost predatory.

"I know, right?" she snapped. "I'm a great actress, remember?"

"Why didn't you just head to Hollywood instead of pursuing a career in finance? You wouldn't have had to fake school transcripts."

She cleared her throat and tightened her hold on her bag. "Too much chance involved. I don't do chance. I do certainty. Control. Something I could work hard enough to achieve. Luck has never really been on my side—" she swept a hand up and down in Eduardo's direction "—obviously. So I didn't figure I should make a plan that included lucking into anything."

"Are you saying our association has been unlucky for you?"

She gritted her teeth, thinking of the letter of recommendation that had happened to find the firm she'd wanted so badly to get a job at in New York. A letter from the HR department at Vega. "Not entirely, but you have to admit, getting kidnapped on your wedding day isn't good luck."

He chuckled as the elevator stopped. "Now, that depends."

The doors slid open and he stepped out; she followed. "On what?"

"On how you feel about the person you're marrying."

The floor was quiet, essentially vacant. The highest offices in the building were reserved for the big dogs of the company, and at this point, Eduardo was the biggest dog.

He opened the door to what had been his father's office, and Hannah's throat constricted. More emotion. She wasn't used to it. She didn't like it, either.

"You don't have to open doors for me, you know," she said, sweeping into the room. "I know you aren't a gentleman."

He arched a brow and closed the door behind them. "I'm hardly trying to convince you otherwise."

"Obviously."

"All right, Hannah," he said, moving to his desk, his demeanor changing. He sat down and hit a few keys on his keyboard, waking up the flat-screen monitor. "This is what we're looking at."

"What's this?"

"Financial records for the past few years."

"I need to sit," she said.

He stood from the computer chair and she slid past him, trying to ignore the little jolt of pleasure she felt when she brushed against him. "So, what exactly do you think is going on?"

He blew out a breath. "Certain things in particular are problematic for me. Remembering numbers and dates are among them. But it wouldn't be as big of an issue had I not hired someone to handle it that didn't do his job."

"On purpose or…criminally?" she asked, opening the report for the previous years' finances.

"I'm not entirely certain."

"Well, incompetence should be criminal," she said, skimming the numbers. "And please hold all comments on how I should be an expert on the matter. I am in here saving your butt, after all."

"You are so very charming, Hannah."

She gritted her teeth and leaned in closer to the computer screen, trying to close him out of her range of focus. "Yeah, well, had I gone to charm school I probably would have failed there just as spectacularly as I flunked out of high school."

"Why did you fail high school? Because we both know you're capable of doing the work."

Her stomach dipped and she tried to will away the gut-tearing pain that always came with this set of memories. Tried to put herself firmly in the present, as Hannah Weston. Not as the Hannah she had been. "I didn't try."

"That doesn't sound like you, either."

"Yeah, well, making stupid financial decisions doesn't sound like you, and yet here we are."

She chanced a look at his face. His expression was hard, his lips set into a grim line. She'd gone too far again. She knew that. But she wasn't opening the door on her past. She just wasn't. She couldn't.

He gripped the arms of the chair and turned her so that she was facing him. "Stupid? Stupid decisions? Is that what you call them?"

"I was making a point." She slid the chair back and stood. The idea was to bring her up to his level. But since her eyes only met his chest, the only point it served to make was that, even in three-inch heels, she was a whole lot smaller than he was.

"Then you won't mind if I make one of my own." He wrapped his arm around her waist and tugged her against him, her breasts coming into contact with his chest. He raised his hand, brushing his shaking thumb over her lip, the gesture shockingly gentle given the heat and anger visible in his eyes.

The rage in him was palpable, satisfying in a way. She'd brought him to the brink with her words. His muscles trembled as he held her. She waited. For his lips to crash down on hers. Rough and painful. The way it often was with men when they lacked control or were just too turned on to think straight. The way it most certainly would be with him so angry.

But there was no crash.

He dipped his head, his lips a breath from hers. The breath fled her body, all her focus diverting to him. He was so close. So tempting. She found her face tilting so that her mouth could meet his, found herself giving in. Giving up.

His lips were hot, firm. And suddenly, he wasn't holding her to him anymore. She'd melted against him. His tongue slid against the seam of her mouth and she opened, heat flooding her, making her core tighten, her breasts feel heavy. He wrapped his other arm around her and she lifted her hands, pressing them on his hard chest.

He angled his head, deepening the kiss, tightening his hold on her. She whimpered and freed her hands, sighing when her breasts met his chest. She wrapped her arms around his neck, threading her fingers through his hair, holding him to her.

He devoured her, and she returned the favor. Never, not in their six months of marriage, had they kissed like this. Nothing more than proprietary pecks for public displays. A slightly more intimate kiss on their wedding day, since they'd had an audience.

But this was just them. Alone. And there was no control. No thought. She hadn't even tried to maintain her hold on either, she'd simply released them, and drowned in his kiss.

Then, just as suddenly as he'd embraced her, he released her, his eyes dark black pits that seemed to draw her in and repel her at the same time. And she realized she didn't have half the hold over him as he did over her.

"The point I was making," he bit out, his tone rough, strained, "is that you might not like me, and you might want to think that I'm somehow stupid, but we both know that I have the power here."

She took in a shaking breath. "You...bastard."

"Don't forget it. I'm not a boy you can manipulate. I'm not the foolish idiot I once was who might have been distracted by a pretty face." He turned away from her, heading out the door. "Let me know what you find."

She didn't answer. She couldn't. As soon as he exited the office she pounded her fist on the desk, letting the sting alleviate the burn of humiliation that had taken over.

She wouldn't let him make a fool of her like that. Never again.

Eduardo drew a shaking hand over his face. He had not meant to do that. He had not meant to touch her, or kiss her. He hadn't meant to lose control.

Rage had been a feral beast inside of him, pushing him,

driving him. Rage, and then, the hot surge of lust that had tipped him over the edge.

His body burned. He'd been so close to pushing her on the surface of the desk and...

He laughed into the empty room and gave thanks for the mostly private floor.

He hadn't touched a woman in five years. Five years of celibacy that he hadn't minded in the least. Now it seemed to be crushing him, five years all added together and suddenly very, very apparent.

It was more than that, though. It was this thing in him that he didn't know. This strain of unpredictability that he couldn't control or anticipate.

He didn't understand the man he'd been. He didn't know, or like, the man he was.

This wasn't how it was supposed to work. She wasn't supposed to appeal to the new, darker side of him. She was supposed to remind him of that light, easy time. Was supposed to bring those feelings back.

Beyond that, he did need her to help straighten out the company's finances, and he could not afford to be distracted. He had to see this through, and he could not afford a distraction. He couldn't afford to divert his focus any more than it already was. He had no control over the effects of his injury. No control over the forgetfulness or the migraines. But he would damn well control his body's reaction to her.

He gritted his teeth and walked back into the office. Hannah jumped and turned.

"Knock for heaven's sake," she growled, turning back to the screen.

"It's my office."

"Well...you left."

"And now I am back."

"Yes, you are," she said, her shoulders rolled forward, her expression intense, focused on the screen. She let out a short breath. "It's not that bad." She turned the chair so that she was facing him, a guarded expression on her face.

"You don't think?"

"No. The fees you incurred for late taxes…I can't help you with that. That was the work of a very sucky employee and I'm glad he's been fired. The rest is manageable. I could recommend some investment and savings strategies and, actually, you're missing a few tax breaks you could take advantage of while making sure your employees get better benefits."

"You make it sound…easy."

"It is," she said. "When it's your area of expertise. Can you explain to me exactly what isn't working for you? I need to know so I can help you get a system in place."

He hated that word. *Help.* He had thought nothing of it before his accident. But then, he hadn't needed it. He was supposed to be the one who provided help, the one people went to. He was the man of the Vega family. He wasn't supposed to need so much.

"Numbers and dates get reversed when I read them. And I have a very hard time remembering them. And my attention span has…shortened. It's hard to sit down and read something for a long time. Harder to retain it."

"Do they think it will ever change?"

He shrugged, like it didn't matter. "Probably not, but it's impossible to know, really."

"You're okay with it?"

A chuckle escaped his lips, not because he felt there was anything funny, but because it seemed the only response he was capable of for a moment. "Would you be okay if you woke up with a brain that wasn't yours? That's how I feel. All the time."

She looked down, her complexion pale. "I've been trying to be someone else for the past nine or ten years. I might not mind."

"Trust me, *querida,* you would. But, either way, I cannot

change what is. So I only concern myself with what can be changed."

She planted both hands on his desk and pushed herself into a standing position. She seemed to have forgotten the kiss, her expression as icy and composed as ever. He still shook inside.

"What I would like to do, is work on implementing a system that will be easier for you to track. Then I want to make sure you find some good, trustworthy financial managers. Not until everything is corrected, you understand."

"You always did think quickly on your feet. Or in an office chair."

Her lips curved into a smile. A real smile, not a smirk or a forced expression. "This is what I do. I'm good at it."

"You always have been. That's why I came to you."

"That and the leverage."

"A man can't go into battle unarmed."

A flicker of heat sparked in her eyes and he knew that she was replaying the kiss. So, she wasn't unaffected. She hadn't brushed it off. But she was right, she was an accomplished actress. She'd gotten even better, even harder to read since the beginning of their sham marriage. He had worried about her breaking character then. Even now, with the little spark visible in the depths of her eyes, he doubted anyone else would see anything beyond the cool, composed beauty she seemed to project. It would keep most people from looking deeper.

She was a petite blonde, well dressed, perfectly coiffed. She had a look that could easily become generic, and might be to some. It was her eyes that showed how different she was. That showed her intelligence, her steel.

She cleared her throat, tilted her chin up. "Well, I doubt anyone would accuse you of that."

"I'm flattered by the assessment."

"Don't be, or I'll have to punch you in the ego again."

"I see, so you're trying to knock me down a couple of pegs in an attempt to gain the upper hand. It won't work. I'm happily absent an ego, in many ways. Social status means little to me. I haven't tried to impress friends or women in so many years I can hardly remember why I ever bothered in the first place. Though, the forgetting could also be a side effect of my head injury."

She shifted, her lips bunching together.

"You don't like it when I joke about my accident?" he asked.

She shrugged. "It's your trauma, man. Deal with it however you want."

"I've dealt with it," he said, his words coming out harsher than intended. Lies. "I've dealt with my father's death, with trying to ensure my mother and sister are happy, well taken care of. And now, I'm dealing with fixing what has fallen into disrepair here at the company."

"And I'm here to help you do it." She arched her pale eyebrows. "Under sufferance, you understand, but I am here. And I am helping."

For some reason, his entire body didn't seize in response to the use of the word.

"You are."

CHAPTER FIVE

HANNAH leaned against the railing on the penthouse terrace and looked down at the city. The sky was dark, stars piercing holes in the blackness, and below, Barcelona was lit. Cars still crowded the road, people headed to restaurants and clubs.

She breathed in deep—warm air filling her lungs. She smelled salt, the sea, but it wasn't the same as it was in San Francisco or New York. Here it seemed spicier, richer. It always had. It had always called to her in a different way. Begged her to strip off her control and let herself go free.

And she had always denied it.

"Having trouble sleeping?"

She turned, her heart catching when she saw Eduardo leaning in the doorway. He'd traded in his work attire for casual black pants and a tight T-shirt that hugged his muscular physique almost as tightly as she'd hugged him earlier in his office.

Don't think about that.

She wouldn't. Not again. That was over. Done. No more kissing. Not in private anyway.

"I'm still a little off. Jet lag and all."

"Tell me, Hannah."

Her throat tightened, strange, irrational fear assaulting her. "Tell you what?"

"Tell me what you've been doing with yourself these past five years."

She almost sighed in relief. Five years she could do. "Working. I was in New York for about three years, working on Wall Street, of all things, then I relocated to San Francisco. I started to get a good client base at the firm I was with, doing personal financial management and investments. I hit a bit of a wall, though, because male bosses, coworkers and clients always seemed to think single meant available. So when I met Zack a year ago, it seemed perfect. I could get married, and I could do my job without so much sexual harassment."

"And that's the only reason you were going to marry him? I hate to be the one to tell you, but men who are inclined to behave that way sexually harass women with wedding rings, too."

"Sure they do, but Zack is influential. Wealthy. It would be a brave man who attempted to poach on his territory."

Eduardo chuckled, dark and enticing. "Like me?"

"Yes. Brave or stupid."

His eyes locked with hers. "Do you remember what happened last time you used that word?"

Heat and regret assaulted her. Heat from the memory of the kiss, regret because she'd insulted him. She wished she felt more regret in regards to the actual kissing.

"I won't do it again."

"Good." He walked to the railing, resting his forearms on the metal surface. He was barefoot. Strange that she noticed. He seemed slightly more human than usual in that moment. "Were you going to have a family with him? Children?"

A shiver started in her stomach, working its way through her. "No. No children."

"You don't want them?"

"No. Never. What would I do with a baby, anyway?" She laughed, as though it were the most ridiculous thing in the world. And she fought hard against the tight, clenching pain in her womb. Against the memories.

"Raise it, I suppose. But then, wearing a baby in a sling

while you're cursing and trading stocks is maybe not that practical."

She swallowed the bile that was rising in her throat. "You want children?"

"No," he said. Just no. Good. She didn't want to talk about her aversion to children, either. Didn't want to open up that box. It held so much fear, and regret and guilt. She just couldn't look in it at the moment. She did her best to never, ever look in it. To never remember.

"Not practical for people like us," she said. She and Zack had had a very similar conversation once. And in his response she'd sensed the same dark grief that she felt hovering around the edges of his answers. Another reason she'd never pressed him for his secrets. She was certain they shared something too similar, too painful. She knew it was why he'd never pressed for hers.

"Of course not."

"We were going to be partners. Help each other out. It's good to have a partner in life."

"I suppose so," he said slowly. "But that isn't how I want to live."

"No?"

"No. I would rather be able to do things independently. If I ever had a wife…I would have wanted to take care of her."

"Not every woman wants to be taken care of." But for a moment she wondered what it would be like. To have someone shoulder some of the pain. To have someone who knew every secret. Who shared every fear. Someone who would cover her, shield her.

A silly thought. She didn't want that. She was the only person she could trust. The only person she could depend on.

"It's how I think things should be done. That's how my parents did things. They were happy."

"How is your mom?"

"Grieving. Still. She spent more than thirty years with my father. His death has been hard for her."

"I'm sorry. Your parents were… They're the only place I've ever seen love, let's put it that way."

"The only place? What about your parents?"

What was the harm in giving him a little? He knew more about her than anyone else. "I don't know. I don't think they ever married. When I was three my mom left me at my dad's single-wide and never came back. She had all my stuff tied up in a little plastic bag. Anyway, he didn't know what to do with a kid. He…he tried I guess. But he was kind of a mess."

He frowned. "Your mother left you?"

"Not every family is perfect. But I don't dwell on it."

"You don't even acknowledge it."

"I lived in this dirty, dusty mobile home. The park it was in had a dirt road and when trucks would drive by, the dirt was like a cloud. It settled on everything. Everything was always dirty. I actually felt lucky to only have one parent. There was no fighting in my house. I could always hear the neighbors screaming at each other. My father never yelled. He just barely ever said hi, either."

She could stay out all night and he'd hardly ever raise an eyebrow when she'd come in at breakfast. She could still see him, sitting in his chair with a bowl of cereal in his lap and a beer already in his hand.

"How were the sheets?" he asked.

"I didn't have any. Just a mattress on the floor and a blanket. We didn't have a washer and dryer so…I used to hitchhike to the Laundromat sometimes so I could clean my blankets and clothes."

She shook her head. "I mean…would you want to talk about that? Who wants that life?"

He frowned. "No one. Is that why you erased your past?"

She swallowed. "One of the many whys. But let's not even get into that." It was one thing to talk about her parents, such as they were. To talk about the things that had been out of her control. The poverty, the neglect. She could handle that.

But she'd made her own mistakes. Those were the ones that stayed closest to her, like a layer over her skin, protective and confining at the same time, impossible to remove. A part of her she wished away every day, and one she depended on to move forward.

"Fine by me." He looked out at the view. "Tell me, Hannah, what is it like to walk away from everything?" His tone was husky, sincere. Surprising.

"I... It's like walking out of prison," she said. "Like I imagine it might be, anyway. You spend all this time in a place you know isn't right, and yet, you have to stay. Until one day, you just walk out into the sunlight. You'd never go back, even though going forward is frightening. Because there's so much possibility when before that...there was nothing."

"How did you end up in Spain? Why Spain?"

Admitting she'd sort of put her finger on the globe in a random place would seem silly. As silly as the fact that she'd chosen her new last name from an upscale department store she'd seen on TV. But that was the truth. She'd been so desperate then, to shed who she was, to try and be someone else. To make something else of herself. "I wanted to get very far away. I wanted out of the country because..."

"It would be easier for you to get away with false transcripts."

"Yes. Of course they were very good, and I had changed my name legally by that point." She didn't know why she was telling him all of this. Only that with him determinedly keeping his focus on the street below, the darkness surrounding them, it seemed easy.

"And where did you get the money for it?"

The fifteen thousand dollars she never wanted to talk about. Fifteen thousand dollars she did her best to *never* think about. It had bought documents; it had supplied her with her plane ticket and passport, ID that carried her new name.

A gift. The money had been a gift, not payment, because how could a price be put on what she'd given? At least, that was what they'd told her. The Johnsons, from somewhere in New Hampshire. The couple she'd given her baby to. Oh, they'd paid all the legal adoption fees, and her hospital bill, but in the end, they'd wanted to do more. To get her on her feet. Provide her with a new start so she didn't end up back in the same place.

They had. They truly had. She should be grateful. She was.

But thinking about it was like drawing her skin off slowly. It still made her feel raw, freshly wounded and bleeding. Still made her ache with guilt. Guilt over everything. That it had ever happened. That she'd made the choice she had. And then there was the guilt that came along with the occasional, sharp sweep of relief that she'd chosen to give the baby up. That she hadn't kept him. That she hadn't spent their lives repeating the cycle her parents had been a part of.

"From a friend," she said. It was a lie. But it was the kind of lie she was used to. The kind of lie that kept all the events from her past glossed over. The kind that kept it hidden away. Kept it from being drawn out into the light and tearing her apart.

"Good friend."

"Oh, yeah. Great friend." She cleared her throat and blinked hard. "And you, Eduardo, what's it like to have a place you can call yours? What's it like to feel at home?" She wished she hadn't asked. It was too revealing. The ache in her voice was so obvious, at least to her own ears.

"I have never thought very much about it, or rather, I never had. Not before. I always took it as my due. Vega was to be mine, my position in both society and my family always sure and set. Now that I know what it's like to feel like a stranger to myself? Well, now I wish I would have appreciated the ease a bit more."

Silence fell between them and she closed her eyes, listening to the traffic below, music coming from somewhere nearby.

"Did we just have a moment?" she asked.

"A what?"

"A moment. Like, a human moment where we talked without fighting or snarking or trying to put each other down."

"I think we did. But we need never speak of it again."

She opened her eyes and looked into his. Even in the dim light, she could see a glimmer of mischief there, something like the old Eduardo.

"It's a deal," she said.

For one moment, her mind went blank of everything. Everything but his face, and what it had been like to be in his arms earlier. What it had been like to kiss him. And in that moment, she couldn't remember why kissing him wasn't a great idea. But just for that one moment.

Then that blank simplicity got crowded out by reality, by the reason why she couldn't kiss him. Not now, not ever.

She wasn't building a life here with him. When this was over, she had to go back home. To her clients, to her job. Assuming Zack wasn't having her blacklisted.

"I'm tired now," she lied. She didn't think she would ever be able to sleep right while she was here. While she knew he was right across the penthouse from her, sleeping. Possibly naked. It hadn't bothered her five years ago. She didn't know what had changed in her since then.

That was a lie. She did know. Eduardo had changed. And there was something about him now that called to her.

She really had to get a grip on herself. And the weak, mushy emotion she seemed to be tempted to wallow in the past few days. She didn't have time, she didn't need to, she didn't want to.

She was Hannah Weston. She was her own invention, her own woman. And she could do this.

"Good night, Eduardo," she said, bringing a little steel back into her tone. "See you at the office tomorrow."

CHAPTER SIX

"YOUR wife is back and you didn't tell your mother?"

Eduardo turned to face Hannah, who was sitting at his desk, holding his phone more tightly to his ear as his mother's voice rang through loudly.

"*Lo siento, Mama.* It happened very suddenly. I have been working at…making amends." Bringing his mother into the charade wasn't ideal, but he would do what had to be done. He'd been avoiding her for weeks. That period of avoidance had clearly ended.

"You've been making amends? For what, Eduardo? She was the one who left you without a word. After six months of marriage. Divorced." She said the word like it was something truly foul.

"Ah, yes, but we were not divorced. We never have been. Hannah and I are as married today as we were that day in the cathedral."

Hannah's focus snapped up from the computer, her blue eyes trained on him, her expression hard. *"What?"* she mouthed.

He covered the mouthpiece on the phone. *"My mother,"* he mouthed back to her.

Then her lips formed a soundless version of a truly filthy word. He chuckled and uncovered the phone.

"We will come to see you this weekend. In fact, let's make it a long weekend at the *rancho*. Bring Selena, of course."

Hannah threw her hands in the air, her eyes round. He offered her a half smile and she put her hands on her throat like she was choking herself, then pointed at him. He suppressed a laugh and listened to his mother's response.

"See you then," he said, cutting off any last protests. She would be there. She would never disappoint him.

"What did you do that for?" Hannah exploded.

"Because, it's what I would do if we were really reconciling, which means it's what we should do in order to make it look like we're reconciling. *Entiende?*"

"No. *No entiendo.* I don't understand at all. Why bother bringing your mom and Selena into this? It's not…fair."

"To them or to you?"

"Either one," she said. "Look, I liked your family—a lot—when I was here. They were really good to me and I hated lying to them. I don't want to do it again."

"You're sparing my mother from the possibility of losing Vega. I think she'll forgive you."

"I'll be honest with you, Eduardo. I don't think you're in danger of losing Vega. Things aren't quite as good as they were a few years ago, but that's true for a lot of companies. And anyway, your personal assets are quite healthy. Once you get your financial manager in place—"

"But if I don't figure out a system…"

"We will," she said, moving into a standing position and grasping her hands behind her back, arching forward, stretching, a short little kitten sound escaping as she did. His body kicked into gear, a hard and serious reminder of the power she seemed to command over him.

Her breasts were perfect. Small and round. He ached to have them in his palms. In his mouth.

"We had better," he bit out, averting his eyes. He had to get a grip. He had other things to worry about, things much more important than his neglected sex drive.

"I'm confident that we can figure something out," she said,

rounding the desk, her hips dipping with each step. She was still angry. Her hips moved more when she was angry, her lips pulled tight. "Now," she breathed out, "do we really have to spend the weekend with your family?"

"Yes. My mother will not let it go…you know it as well as I do. And I think it would do us both good to get out of the city."

"It's only been a few weeks. And anyway, I like the city, so I feel no such need."

"Ah, but you do." He started to circle her. Her head swiveled as far as it possibly could as she tried to track his movement. He put his hands on her shoulders, savoring the heat of her body coming through her thin top. "You're very tense." He moved his thumb into her muscle and discovered that tense was an understatement.

"Ow," she groused.

"You will feel better in a moment." He moved his thumb on the other side, digging deeper. She arched back, whimpering.

"It doesn't feel better yet."

"Your muscles are like rocks. It doesn't help that you hunch at the computer."

"Shut up, I do not hunch."

"You do." He worked both of her shoulders until he felt some of the tightness ease, until she stopped fidgeting and started melting into his touch. He swept her blond hair to the side and slid his thumb up the back of her neck. This time, the sound she made was decidedly pleased, and more than a little bit sexy.

"Yes, just like that," she said, arching into his touch, instead of trying to escape it.

"I do like to hear you say that," he said. He tilted his head to the side and pressed a kiss just beneath her earlobe. She stiffened, then pulled away from him.

"I'm still mad at you," she said, turning to face him, her eyes looking a little glazed, her cheeks flushed.

"That's okay. It doesn't mean you can't kiss me. You were mad at me last time, too."

She drew her plump lower lip between her teeth and shook her head. "Nope. Not kissing you."

"Why not?"

"Because it's not what we're here to do."

She was right. He knew it. And until he'd touched her again, he'd firmly believed it. There was too much at stake for him in so many ways. And yet he couldn't find it in him to suppress the desire. "That's true. But mixing a little pleasure in with business doesn't have to be detrimental."

"Maybe not, but it usually is."

"Speaking from experience."

"No, I'm way too smart for that. I keep business and personal very, very separate. And you, my dear, are business. Always have been."

She was lying. He extended his hand and drew his finger along the curve of her cheek, felt her tremble beneath his touch. Now *she* knew she was lying, too.

"We'll finish up work for the day, and when we get back to the penthouse, we'll get ready to drive to the *rancho* first thing in the morning."

Eduardo owned a Jeep, which surprised her almost as much as his insistence they make the drive out of Barcelona and into the countryside with the top down.

But the air was warm and the scenery was beautiful, so she wasn't going to complain. Even though her hair was whipping around so violently she nearly swallowed a chunk of it. She tugged the strands from her lips and shook her head, hoping to get it somewhat back into place.

"I don't think I ever came out here with you...before, I mean," she said, competing with the wind and the engine.

"No. This is new. I bought it after my accident. I liked

going to a place where I could think. Somewhere away from the city and…people."

"You have horses?"

He nodded, his eyes never leaving the road. "Yes. I don't ride them."

"You don't?"

"No."

"I assume you have staff that do?"

"Of course. And you know Selena is really into horses."

"I remember. She must be…not a teenager anymore." She remembered Eduardo's younger sister, all long skinny limbs, round eyes and glossy hair. She'd been fifteen when Hannah had seen her last, but she would be twenty now. A woman, not a girl.

"No, she's not."

"Strange because it doesn't feel like it's been that long since… Well, in some ways. There are times when it feels like this was part of another lifetime. And like I'm in an alternate dimension now."

"It's very possible, I suppose. Maybe I'm in one, too, and I'll wake up with a throbbing headache and my memory fully restored."

"Click your heels together and say 'there's no place like home.'"

"*Qué?*"

"Dorothy. *The Wizard of Oz.* You don't know that movie? Everyone knows that movie."

He shook his head. "I've seen it. I…didn't remember the reference."

An uneasy silence fell between them, her stomach tightening as the meaning of his statement settled in. "If I clicked my heels together," she said, "and said that, I wonder where I would end up? Maybe in the middle of nowhere."

"You don't have a home?"

"Right now I have an apartment in San Francisco. But is

it home? I don't know about that." She looked down at her hands. "Sometimes I think it would be a blessing to have a little memory loss."

"Was it that bad?"

Unbidden, she thought about what it had felt like to have her baby move inside of her. Of the moment he'd been delivered. Of having to turn away as the nurse carried him from the room so that she wouldn't have time to memorize his tiny, perfect face.

She had it memorized anyway. One moment was enough. And not enough.

She tried to breathe past the tightness in her chest. "Some things really are that bad."

"I've forgotten a great many things that didn't matter. But I don't know they don't matter. And that's the worst part. You're not sure if you've forgotten something trivial, or vital. A lot of the time I'm unsure if I've forgotten anything at all. I could neglect an important document and never once have that nagging feeling you count on having to keep you on track."

She redirected her thoughts, pulling the door closed on her memories, on her emotions, locking it tight. "Have you set up alerts?"

"What kind?"

"You could have them on your phone, your computer. We could sync them up so you could be reminded at different times of the day that certain things need doing."

"I don't forget everything," he said, his tone rough.

"I know that. But you don't always know what will slip your mind, do you? So you have to be willing to put down your pride for a little bit and cover your bases. This isn't about hanging on to your manly image."

"The hell it's not," he grumbled.

"Eduardo." She sighed. "Get over yourself."

"Why would I want to do that? I am so wonderful." He tossed her a smile and for a moment, the heaviness in her lightened. For the rest of the trip, they kept the topics neutral, choosing to avoid anything real or personal.

When they pulled off the main road and onto a winding, single-lane paved road that wound up the mountain, Hannah tried not to show any nerves.

"You're bothered by heights?" he asked.

"Oh, only a little," she said. She hated to show fear, of any kind. Especially a silly fear of heights. "I mean, if another car came around the corner our only options are the side of the mountain and plummeting to our doom."

"I promise to keep the plummeting to a minimum."

"Appreciated," she said tightly.

She breathed a sigh of relief when the road curved in, away from the drop and through a thick grove of trees. It was cool, green and lush, shaded from the heat of the day.

The trees thinned and faded until they were surrounded by green fields, stretching to the mountains on one side, and to the edge of a cliff on the other, overlooking the brilliant, jewel-bright sea.

Large iron gates secluded the property from the rest of the world. Eduardo used an application on his phone to enter in the code and the gates swung open.

"I use letters in my security code," he said as they drove on. "They're easier for me to remember. I'm not sure why."

"I'm not, either. I would have to do some reading on the subject."

The house was set back into the property, nearer to the sea, bold floor-to-ceiling windows reflecting the sun. It was an angular, modern house with traditional white stucco and a red ceramic tile roof. A mix of the old and new, very like its owner.

"This is beautiful," she said. "Quiet, too."

"Away from the noise," he said. "For a while I badly needed that. Things are better now than they were."

"I'm glad to hear that."

"I still prefer to be here. Alone."

"That's very unlike you. You used to drag me to parties all the time. Parties with music so loud we rarely had to talk to anyone. And if I didn't go, you went by yourself."

"I used to like that sort of thing. I don't now." He pressed another button on his phone and a door to the large garage opened, and he pulled the car inside.

"Very techie," she said.

"It makes my life easier."

"And I'm sure we can come up with even more ways to make it easier on you. Why haven't you seen anyone about this before?"

His body tensed. "I saw doctors."

"I know, but have you ever gone to programmers or anything with a list of your specific issues? I'm almost certain there are some simple…"

"No. I'm not spreading this around for the world to see. I'll not be made to look like a fool. Or stupid," he said, his dark gaze pointed on hers. He looked down at his hands. "Tell me something, Hannah."

"What?"

"Why did I like going to all those parties?"

"What?" she asked.

"Why did I like them? The idea of going to parties…now it seems like it would be loud and…confusing. I can't imagine what it was that made me like them before and sometimes I think if I could just remember…then I could make myself feel it again."

Hannah's stomach tightened. "Eduardo…I…" She took a breath. "You liked to be around people. To have them see you. You always commanded the room and you…thrived on that."

He rested his head on the back of the seat. "I still can't…" He let out a long breath. "I can't feel it now."

He killed the engine and slammed the driver's-side door shut, skipping the chivalry and walking straight into the house alone. She unbuckled and followed him out of the Jeep and into the house.

Yet again, the luxury available to the Vega family floored her. She was no slouch, and she made a darn decent income, but this was beyond the everyday version of luxury.

Sweeping vistas of the sea, intensely green fields and mountains, marble floors and a grand, curving staircase. Light poured in, light everywhere, making it feel like she was still outdoors, bringing the natural beauty into the man-made extravagance.

She pulled her lips tight, doing her very best not to look impressed. "Eduardo…I'm going to get lost in this palace without a guide." She was determined to change the subject. Determined to ignore the pain in her chest. His pain.

He came into the entryway, his expression neutral. So she wasn't the only one trying to play a game, trying to hide her feelings. "I will happily give you the tour." There was a glimmer in his eyes, one she didn't like at all. She had a feeling he was about to do something to make her angry, since that seemed to be the only thing that made him laugh these days.

"What?" she asked, following him up the curving staircase. "And shouldn't I go get my bags?"

"I don't know what you mean, and one of my staff will have your bags delivered to the room later."

"You know what I mean. You look amused, and that never bodes well for me. And *the* room?"

"Yes. The room. Our room."

So that was the cause of the glitter. "Our room? I do hope you're having a malfunction with your English, darling."

"No malfunction, I speak English as well as you do. But we're selling a reconciliation here, and we can hardly sleep across the hall from each other."

She sputtered. "You…you…"

"Relax, *querida,* I'm giving us rooms that connect to each other. I'm not so base as to try and force you to share a bed with me. Still, we will have to be careful that it's not suspected you aren't sleeping with me."

She made a face at him. "You did that just to make me mad."

"I have to confess, it is one of my few joys in life. To watch the color rise in your cheeks." He paused at the top of the stairs and turned to face her, his eyes dark, assessing. Far too assessing. "I love to watch you lose control."

"I did not lose control. You couldn't make me lose control," she said, realizing she sounded childish and very much on the edge of control. Unable to stop it.

He chuckled and turned away from her. "If you say so."

"I do," she muttered, crossing her arms beneath her breasts and trailing behind him, down the expansive half floor, open to the living area below. There were two dark double doors at the end of the hall, and he opened them to an impressive luxury suite.

"I trust you will find this suitable. This is, of course, my room. And that is the door to yours." He indicated a door on the far end of the room. She passed him, her eyes resting longingly on the massive king-size bed piled high with silk pillows, and went to the other door.

She turned the knob and opened it, revealing a smaller, but no less impressive suite.

The bed wasn't as grand, the linen white with pink ribbon edging the bottom of the bedspread, and tied around the throw pillows, making them look like little gifts.

The walls were white, the floors a pale marble, decorated with fuzzy-looking pink carpets.

"It's so pink," she breathed, hating in some ways how perfect it was.

"It's not quite as edgy as you are, I confess."

She turned and saw Eduardo leaning in the door. A giggle bubbled in her throat when she realized that he'd probably imagined she would hate it. But he hadn't seen her very,

very pink wedding cake, or the pink bows she'd selected to go on all of the chairs. He'd never seen her pink dishes in her kitchen, or the pink bed set in her room.

"I happen to love pink," she said, smiling sweetly. "My room when I was a teenager was very..." Dirty. Dark. Depressing. "It wasn't to my taste and I used to dream of decorating my own place as feminine and frilly and bright as I liked. So as soon as I could, I did. It's something I've never grown out of, alas."

One dark brow shot up. "I never would have guessed that about you."

"No, I doubt anyone would. But my life is not an open book."

"I have noticed that."

"Now you know my deep, dark secret. Beneath my ass-kicking facade, I have a thing for ruffles." She liked that she'd caught him off guard. It was a small thing, but she took more than a little pleasure in it.

He shook his head. "Now that is interesting."

"I live to interest."

"I seriously doubt that."

"You're right. I don't care enough about what people think." That wasn't true, either. She wished it was. "What's the thread count on the sheets?"

"I can't remember *The Wizard of Oz*. You think I'll remember that?"

The corner of her mouth tugged up in a reluctant half smile. "Fine, I'll read the tags when you leave."

"I think my mother and Selena will be here soon. If you'd like to dress for dinner."

"Is there something wrong with the way I'm dressed?"

"Do you own anything that's not designed to fit into a boardroom environment?"

"Pink pajamas."

"And now that no longer surprises me, but you can't wear that for dinner, either."

"Yes, I have some other clothes."

"Good. Then I'll have your things sent up." He turned away, then stopped. "Hannah, try to relax. You can think of this as a vacation."

CHAPTER SEVEN

"I DON'T take vacations."

Eduardo turned at the sound of Hannah's voice.

She was at the foot of the stairs, wrapped tightly in a black, knee-length dress, her blond hair loose for once, cascading over her shoulders in an elegant wave. She shifted, her expression tight, painted red lips pulled into a pucker.

"Why does that not surprise me?"

"I hear you don't take them anymore, either."

He shook his head. "I've no inclination to. I often work from here."

"Is it easier? Less distraction?"

He nodded slowly. He'd never really thought of it in those terms. He'd just thought he liked the quiet now, when before he'd thrived in the frenetic pace of the city. He'd enjoyed staying up late and getting up for work the next day. Had liked being surrounded by constant motion and high energy.

He didn't now. He liked solace. Privacy. Order. When there was no order his brain was utter chaos. He'd realized and adjusted for that early on.

"I suppose so. Plus, it's nice to avoid the stares. I'm the accident people can't help but gawk at, after all. Rich playboy, victim of a horrible, unfortunate incident. The public very often enjoy seeing people brought down."

"I don't see you as being brought down. Things are just different, that's all."

Her words, spoken from tight lips, with stilted, stubborn confidence, did something to him. To his chest. His heart. It was strange. Hannah wasn't looking at him with pity, far from it. She seemed to disdain him, but she also believed in him. Not out of obligation or caring, but because she simply did.

It was more valuable in some ways than the confidence shown him by his mother and sister. More valuable than he cared to acknowledge.

Are you so weak you need validation from a woman who would happily spit on you?

No. He wasn't. He was Eduardo Vega, and someday, all of him would remember that. And what that meant.

He heard an engine, tires on gravel. "They're here. Time to play loving couple."

"And dodge verbal barbs," Hannah grumbled, moving to stand next to him. She kept a thin line of space between their bodies. She didn't want to touch him, and that bothered him.

Because she needed to, needed to be comfortable with him if they were to look like a reconciling couple.

He slid his arm around her waist and she stiffened for a moment before relaxing beneath his touch. "They still think our marriage was real, and they need to think it's real now. Remember, we are deliriously happy to be back together."

"We should write that down," she whispered. "It keeps slipping my mind."

"We can't both start forgetting things, Hannah. We'll be in serious trouble if neither one of us can remember what's going on."

He felt her frame jolt with shocked laughter.

"That's better," he said.

Hannah steeled herself for the invasion of Eduardo's family. It wasn't going to be easy, and why should it be? She'd lied to them. So had Eduardo. They both deserved a little contempt. Of course, she was the only one who would get any.

The door opened and Carmela walked in, followed by

Selena. Both women were dressed in a flamboyant yet sophisticated manner, complete with gloves that extended to their elbows and hats with wide brims.

"*Hola,* Eduardo," Selena said, striding forward. Eduardo released Hannah and leaned forward, embracing his sister.

When they parted, Selena eyed Hannah as if unsure of how to receive her or what to say. Hannah very much felt the same unease.

Carmela hung back.

"Hello," Hannah said, calling on all of her nerve, wondering why it was hard. Why she cared. Normally, she could turn off fear, and embrace control. Could put on an easy, charming persona that made everyone feel at ease. Just like she could turn into a pit bull in business negotiations. She swallowed. "It's good to see you again. I'm…pleased to be back. Pleased to be here with Eduardo and…both of you."

Carmela nodded stiffly. "If he is happy to have you, then so are we. No more must be said on the subject. There will be no anger. Come, I am hungry." She led the way into the dining area and Selena followed. Eduardo held back, and Hannah followed his lead.

"If she says she's not going to be angry, she won't be. You can unclench."

Hannah let out a breath. "I'm sorry, I feel like a jerk. I can't believe you're making me do this to your family. Again. How do you look in the mirror?"

For a moment, Eduardo's expression was unguarded, his dark eyes stripped of their shields. It was an expression of cold, deep fear. It was one she could relate to. The kind of fear that lived deep in her, waiting to wrap its icy hands around her throat at the first opportunity. The kind she ran from every day.

"It helps that I hardly recognize the man looking back at me," he said, his voice rough. "I am doing what I must. I cannot fail."

And she knew then, that this wasn't about the media, but

about him. About proving he was still who he used to be, even though it was so clear he wasn't. The question he'd asked her in the car swam through her mind, made her stomach twist. His desire to understand who he'd been, to try and take himself back there.

To make himself something else.

But it echoed in her. She knew it. Understood it. Lived it every day. The need to be more than who she was. Although, while she was terrified she'd someday morph back into who she'd been, he was afraid he would never be the same.

"I will make sure you don't," she said, the vow coming from deep inside of her, from a core of emotion she hadn't realized she still possessed.

He nodded once, wrapped his arm around her waist and guided her into the dining room.

Hannah sank slowly into the warm water of the in-ground hot tub, her knotted muscles protesting the attempt at forced release.

She was stressed. Stressed was a normal state for her so she was rarely aware of it, but she darn well was now. Dinner with Eduardo's family had been difficult. Going to their room, knowing there would be much speculation had been even worse. Which was why, at eleven o'clock, she'd given up any hope of sleeping, even in her princess bed, and had dug in her bags until she'd produced her black, one-piece swimsuit.

She did need a vacation. But not here. Not with Eduardo. Not for the first time, she wondered about Zack. It was weird how much she didn't miss him. She was starting to be thankful, really thankful, they hadn't gotten married.

Still, she felt bad. She draped her arm over the edge of the hot tub and grabbed her phone, which was close by, as always. She fired off a quick message to him before she could think better of it.

It only took a few minutes for a message to ping back.

Fine. I'm with Clara.

Clara was Zack's best friend and business partner. Hannah had been, on a couple of occasions, slightly jealous of the other woman. She'd had a piece of Zack Hannah had never been able to tap into. A piece of him she hadn't wanted to try and tap into, truth be told. Well, he'd taken Clara on their honeymoon, which was proof of how special she was to him.

Maybe…maybe it had turned into something more? She wasn't usually a squishy romantic, but it really helped to think of Zack finding someone else. Someone better.

Are you having a good time?

It was inane and stupid to ask, but she did care.
His reply came a moment later.

Better than I imagined.

She found herself smiling.

I hope you're happy. Happier than you would have been with me.

She hesitated before hitting Send, then took a breath and pressed it.
A reply pinged back.

You be happy, too.

She laughed.

Okay.

She hit Send one last time and put the phone down. Happy. What was that anyway? She'd always thought of it as something she'd reach the farther away she got from Arkansas. The further away she got from the moment the nurses had whisked her baby from the room and handed him to another woman. That the more she made, the more status she gained, the closer it would bring her there. None of it ever seemed to be enough, though. She never seemed closer to happy.

"Do you ever sleep?"

Hannah turned to see Eduardo standing there, dressed in black swim shorts, his chest bare. She almost swallowed her tongue. He was the single most beautiful man she'd ever seen. Well-defined pecs, covered with a fine dusting of dark hair. His abs...she had the completely unbidden thought that it would be heaven to run her fingers over the ripple of muscle. Not just her fingers. Maybe her tongue, too.

Gah! Where had that come from?

"I don't sleep much," she said. Her thighs trembled a little bit when he took a step toward her and she realized, stupidly late, that he was probably planning on getting into the hot tub with her.

"Neither do I." He rounded the hot tub and descended the steps, the water covering his muscular thighs, lean hips, up to his belly button. Not that she was watching with rapt attention. No.

She edged away, trying to put some distance between them, trying to do it subtly. "Yeah, well, I'm always on red alert. Thinking about all the things I have to do at work, stuff like that."

"About your ex-fiancé?"

"Uh, funny you should mention him. I just texted him. He took another woman on our honeymoon so hopefully he's doing all right."

"That doesn't bother you?"

"I actually know her. She's a friend of his, so it could be platonic. But if not...well, I sort of hope it's not. I want him to be happy."

"And the idea of your ex-lover with another woman doesn't…doesn't make you angry?"

Hannah cleared her throat. "Zack was never my lover."

To his credit, Eduardo's face remained unreadable. "I find that hard to believe."

"Yeah, I figured you would. That was why I never corrected you before. Frankly, I don't really care what you think of it, but it is true."

"Why is that?"

"Why weren't we lovers?"

"Yes."

"We weren't in love. I didn't want him to use me. So I figured if we waited on that until after the wedding…no danger." It wasn't entirely true, but she was hardly giving him the whole truth about her sex life. It wasn't his business anyway.

"I don't believe that, Hannah. You don't seem like the sort of woman who could be used. You're far too hard and savvy for that."

She shrugged, her shoulders rising from the warm water, the night air biting them. "All right then, why do you suppose I didn't sleep with him?"

"You like control too much. So making him wait gave you control."

She rolled her eyes and leaned her head back. "You make it sound like I was leading him around by the—" She popped her head back up and met Eduardo's mocking gaze. "I wasn't. That wasn't why. But yeah, maybe control a little bit. Just not like you mean it."

"I understand control, Hannah, wanting it, going to great lengths to keep it. You hardly have to justify yourself to me."

"I feel like I do when you look at me like that. It's your superpower. I never justify myself to anyone. But with you, I do, a little bit."

"Too bad it's a superpower that's of no use to me."

"Thanks," she said, smiling at him. A big fake smile.

He sighed and sat down, draping his arms over the back of the hot tub. She was across the tub from him and she still felt hotter. Felt like she was way too close to him.

"So," she said. "Did your mom say terrible things about me in those few minutes you hung back in the dining room with her?"

"No. She said she wants me to be happy. Just like she said in front of you."

Hannah sighed. "She's a better person than I am. I would hate me."

"If someone did that to your son?"

Hannah's heart dropped into her stomach. "I...I'll never know. I don't have a son. I don't want children." It sounded slightly panicked, and not the least bit cool. But she didn't want to think about it. Didn't want to get anywhere near the topic.

"So you've said."

"Yes, well, I'm saying again." And now she sounded defensive.

"Who hurt you, Hannah?" he asked, pushing off from the wall and walking to the middle of the tub. His chest gleamed in the light from the house, bronzed and muscular. He looked like the angel of death, trying to confront her with the thing she feared most.

"I already told you. My parents sucked."

"But that's not it, I think."

He drew closer, knelt down in front of her, his eyes level with hers. "What happened?"

She couldn't stand it. The concern on his face, in his tone. Couldn't deal with the slow ache it caused in her heart. "Why the hell do you care? You won't remember it twenty minutes after I tell you."

His hand shot out, gripping the back of the hot tub; his eyes blazed with heat. Anger, certainly, and something else. The anger she could handle; it was the else that scared her.

He lifted his other hand, cupped her chin. "Why do you do that?"

"Do what?" she asked, jerking her face away.

"Why do you lash out? Is it when I get too close?"

"What? What does that mean?"

"You can be so pleasant, I've seen it. And then you can put all your shields up and go on attack. I think it's when I start to get close to the truth. And it scares you."

Yes, it scared her to her soul. She wanted to deny it, and she couldn't, because she was trembling inside. But being angry was so much easier than being afraid. And pushing someone away was so much easier when she was being mean.

She pressed her back against the wall, trying to put some more distance between them. "Maybe I'm just not a nice person. Did you ever consider that?"

"I don't think that's the case. I've been accused of being a terrible, boring bastard the past few years. But I don't think that's your problem."

"Maybe you just aren't very good at reading people."

He shook his head. "An interesting gift, or rather, strange side effect, of my injury. I do not surround myself with so much noise, so it seems I have more time, more of an ability to look closely at the people who are around me. You aren't mean, Hannah. You're afraid. The question is, what are you afraid of?"

Her heart was pounding, her body hyperaware of his nearness. She took a breath and pushed off from the wall, standing so that he was slightly beneath her. She put her hand on the back of his neck.

"I'm not afraid of anything," she said, lying. Boldly. Her hands were shaking, her body was shaking. But she couldn't let him win. Couldn't let him see any weakness. Couldn't let him see her.

He took his hand off the wall and put it on the small of

her back, his fingers rough, hot against her skin. Steam rose between them and stirred when she breathed out.

"Is that so?" he asked.

In response she dipped her head, brushing his lips with hers. A hard zip of attraction punched her, deep in her core. He wrapped his other arm around her, his hand splayed between her shoulder blades. She wrapped her arms around his neck and leaned down, deepening the kiss as much as she could in her position.

Her brain was screaming that she was making a mistake. Walking into danger.

Her body was complaining that she wasn't walking fast enough.

She'd been out to prove a point, but everything, the previous conversation, the reason behind her action, was shrouded in the mist that curled between them, that seemed to have wrapped itself around her mind, shielding her in a blessed haze where all that mattered was the feel of his hard body against hers, the feel of his mouth covering hers.

He lowered his hand slowly, cupping the curve of her butt, down to her thigh, tugging gently. She followed his lead, lowering herself so she was straddling his legs, the hard ridge of his arousal apparent, thick and tempting between them.

He pulled her hard against him and she let her head fall back as he kissed her neck, her collarbone. His mouth so hot on her wet skin, warming her where the night air had left her cold.

"Oh, yes," she said, rocking against him, seeking out the pleasure she knew he could provide. Pleasure she knew would far surpass any sexual experience she'd had before.

She tightened her hold on him, claimed his mouth again, her tongue delving deep, his returning the favor, exploring, creating a delicious friction that made her internal muscles tighten.

She could lose herself in him. In this. Close out everything and embrace the passion. The moment. The need to have him deep inside of her, thrusting hard and deep, mirroring the action of his tongue.

She wanted to surrender. To her feelings. Her body's needs. To him.

She wanted to give him her control.

Panic hit her, hard in the breast and she pushed at his chest, trying to free herself from his embrace. He slowly released his hold on her, his expression confused, hazy. She stumbled back, splashing water up around them, and climbed up the side of the hot tub, not bothering to get around him by using the stairs.

"No, this isn't happening," she said, panic clawing at her. Mocking her. Reminding her that she wasn't brave, that she wasn't different. That if she let go, all of the trappings, everything she'd built for herself, would fall away and reveal who she really was. The stupid girl, needy girl. Ready to give it all up so someone would just pay attention to her for a minute. For a few hours. So that she could have someone look at her like she mattered. Forget what she wanted. Forget self-esteem, self-respect. Control.

"I think it is. It has," he said. "It seems to keep happening."

She shook her head. "No. I'm not sleeping with you."

"Oh, so what was that then? Another effort on your part to keep a man controlled? To lead him around by his balls?"

"If you didn't think with them, it wouldn't work so well," she shot back, dying inside. She felt like her defenses were crumbling, like all of her armor was melting from the heat of Eduardo's touch. And she couldn't allow that.

"Perhaps I was wrong, Hannah. Perhaps I was looking for more where more did not exist."

"I told you." She turned and grabbed a towel from one of the lounge chairs, wrapping it around her body. A physical barrier in the absence of a much-needed emotional one.

"You did. Understand this, though—unlike your ex, I will not be a part of your games. You will not play with me."

"You just let me." She turned on her heel and walked out of the courtyard, leaving a trail of wet footprints behind her.

She climbed up the stairs, towel clutched tightly to her chest. She opened the door to her room and closed it firmly behind her, leaning against it. Then she put her hand over her mouth and muffled a sob.

She slid down to her knees, her body shaking as she gave in to tears for the first time in more years than she could count.

Eduardo knocked on the door that connected his room to Hannah's. He had a feeling he would regret checking on her. He shouldn't care what she was feeling. She'd played him. She'd tried to use her body to control him; she'd insulted him.

And yet, he found he still didn't believe it was her. Still didn't believe she was being genuine. She had been afraid. Not just when he'd asked her about her past, she'd been afraid when they'd kissed. Of the passion that had flared up between them.

He felt wild. He didn't feel like himself, whoever the hell that was. And looking at Hannah, touching Hannah, didn't take him back. It took him somewhere else entirely. He had no idea what to do with that.

He knew what he wanted. And for now, wanting something, needing, that was enough.

She didn't answer. He let out a growl and opened the door without waiting for a response.

He saw her, sitting against the wall, her knees drawn up to her chest, her head down. She looked like a broken doll.

"Hannah?" he asked, a pang hitting him hard in the chest.

She raised her head, and he saw tears shining on her cheeks, illuminated by the moonlight. She wiped her cheek with her arm. "Go away."

He took a step toward her. He didn't know what it was that

compelled him when it came to this woman. He didn't know why she felt so imbedded in him, and yet, she did. A part of him he couldn't escape, a part he couldn't forget.

He hadn't wanted to pursue anyone since his accident. He'd had no focused sexual desire.

But Hannah, tough as nails Hannah, who liked pink, who was sitting on the floor now, wet, still in her bathing suit, all her armor stripped, looking like she would shatter if he touched her, she drew him.

She had fascinated him back when they'd first met. A scrappy, low-class, determined girl who had clawed her way up from nothing, just to get an education. To try and change her life. But the fascination had changed. It was different now. Deeper. As though she'd burrowed beneath his skin.

"Are you all right?" he asked.

She pushed up from the floor and stood. He expected her to yell at him. To insult him. Because he'd caught her feeling vulnerable, and that was what she did when he spotted a crack in her armor.

Instead she just straightened, blond hair flicking over her shoulders like a silvery wave, her chin tilted upward. She was like a proud queen, one who would never acknowledge what he'd just witnessed. She would pretend to be above it, above him, if she had to, in order to protect herself. To keep herself securely locked in her ivory tower.

"Of course."

She would never take sympathy from him, and he didn't like seeing her broken. "You owe me an apology, Hannah," he said, changing tactics, hardening his tone.

She tipped her chin up. "For?"

A smile curved his lips, heat pooling in his gut as he stepped toward her. "You insulted me. Good manners dictate you tell me you're sorry."

"But I'm not."

It was a bad idea to push her. It had been a bad idea to

come to her room in the first place. "Perhaps I can change your mind."

She took a step toward him. "I doubt it."

"I don't."

Hannah sucked in a deep breath, tried to erect a barrier between herself and the dark sensuality radiating from Eduardo.

She hated how she shook when she was near him. How much her body ached for his. She hadn't had sex in nine years. Pathetic, but true. All because of fear. All because she was afraid that if she ever let herself lose control, she would find out that she had never changed. It was why she lashed out at him, it was why she ran from him.

She hated fear. Hated how much of it lived inside of her. She'd bought into her own lie of strength. Had done for years. She'd found someone who hadn't challenged her, who hadn't tapped into any sort of deep sexuality, who hadn't worked at uncovering her secrets, and she'd been able to pretend. Pretend that nothing had ever happened to her, that she had never been Hannah Mae Hackett. High school dropout, pregnant teenager, fraud.

With Eduardo, she couldn't pretend.

With Eduardo she couldn't hide the fear, not from him, not from herself. He stripped her with one look. And his touch...

It had to stop. She wouldn't be afraid. She could still have control, even in this. She had to.

She took another step toward him and put her hand on his face. He reached up, wrapped his fingers around her wrist. "Do not test me, Hannah, not again. I am not playing games. If you kiss me, you had better intend to follow through."

"Or what?"

He chuckled. "I would never hurt you. Would never force myself on you. But I will never allow you to touch me again, either. I do not play. If you turn back now, nothing will happen between us."

"I don't intend to turn back," she said.

"Then why did you earlier?"

"Because this is a very, very bad idea. I thought I would turn back while I still could." Now if she turned back she would be doing it because of fear, and she would know that was why. But if she kissed him… She could do it now. While she had him off guard. While she was in command.

He turned her hand and pressed a kiss to the underside of her wrist, his dark eyes never leaving hers.

"Why don't you kiss me?" she asked.

"Why don't you apologize?"

A laugh escaped, nervous. Strange sounding. "I might feel more sorry if you just give me what I ask for."

He hesitated for a moment, dark eyes glittering. Then he dipped his head, his mouth claiming her quickly, fiercely. She didn't want anything intruding, no thoughts, no emotions; she only wanted what he made her feel. The intense ache that he brought to her core, the desire to have him, over her, in her.

She ran her hands down his bare chest, relishing the feel of his muscles beneath her palms. She'd never touched a man who looked like him, had never been with a real man, truly. Fumbling teenage boys who didn't know what foreplay meant hardly counted as comprehensive sexual experiences.

They hadn't been the complete sensual playground that Eduardo was. He was so masculine, so perfectly formed.

She felt her breath getting short, choppy, and she slowed it, taking a few steadying breaths to help reset the rhythm. To keep herself from losing her mind.

She had the control here. He wanted her; she could see the hunger in his lean face. She held the power.

He moved his hands up her waist, kissing her deeply, thoroughly, his thumbs skimming the undersides of her breasts. She moaned into his mouth and an answering sound of pleasure reverberated in his chest.

He slid his hands higher, cupping her, teasing her nipples. A shot of pure, liquid heat poured into her core. She put her hands on his butt and drew him tighter against her, his erection pressing hard against her hip.

He gripped one of the straps on her swimsuit and tugged it down, dropping a kiss onto her shoulder, peeling the Lycra away from her skin, exposing her breast. "Oh, yes. So beautiful," he said, his voice rough, pained.

He lowered his head, his tongue caressing her nipple, circling it before he sucked it deeply into his mouth. She raised one hand quickly, fisting his hair, holding him to her. He lowered her other strap, baring her other breast. He moved his attention there, lavishing it with the same, very thorough attentions.

She closed her eyes, the sheer intensity of the desire rocketing through her making it impossible to move. Impossible to breathe. Impossible to do anything but stand there and just let him have his way with her body.

When he gripped her swimsuit and pulled it down the rest of the way, a flash of panic hit her. But it was dark. He wouldn't be able to see. Wouldn't notice the silvery lines that trailed over her stomach.

Even if he did, it didn't mean he would know what they were.

He sucked harder on her breast while he teased the other one with his thumb and that last conscious thought fled.

He raised his head and kissed her mouth again, his hair-roughened chest providing the stimulation now.

"Yes, yes," she repeated, over and over, mindlessly as he backed her to the bed and lowered her onto the soft surface.

Dimly, she remembered that she was supposed to take control, that this was about proving that she wasn't afraid, that she could master her need for him, and hold him in the palm of her hand.

The only part that registered was the last one.

She reached down between them and touched at the apex

of his thighs with her hand, moving her palm over the hard ridge of his shaft.

A little tremor of fear shot through her. Fear of pain. It had been a long time. And it had never been with a man like him.

"I… Do you have condoms?" she asked, a trickle of panic hitting her. She shook it off. She wasn't going to let fear have anything in her anymore. Wouldn't let it have anything in this.

He swore. "Just a moment."

He rose from the bed and walked out of the room. She scooted to the center of the mattress, reclining against the pillows. Some of the arousal fog cleared without him there, touching her and kissing her.

It was too late to turn back now. If she did, it would be because of fear, and she wasn't going to let fear have a foothold anymore.

But she was taking the control back. She wasn't letting him turn her into a mindless pleasure zombie. That was her job.

He returned a few moments later, a box in hand. "It was in the bathroom. What conscientious staff I have."

"You didn't know if they were in there?"

"I have not needed them." He set the box down on the nightstand and tore it open, taking out a condom packet. And then she forgot to ask him why he hadn't needed them.

He handed the condom to her and she got up onto her knees, scooting to the edge of the bed. She swallowed hard and hooked her fingers in the waistband of his swim trunks, the damp fabric clinging to his body and she dragged it downward.

When she'd gotten the shorts off, she took him into her hand, reveling in the hot, silky skin, the hardness of him. She squeezed him lightly and he groaned, the sound deep and satisfying.

"You are certainly no ordinary man," she said. He let his head fall back, a raw groan coming from deep inside of him.

"That's right, Eduardo," she whispered. "Let me." A straight shot of power coursed through her, making her feel fearless.

She lowered her head and flicked the tip of her tongue over his shaft, her stomach tightening with desire as his hand came up to her head, his fingers tangling in her hair. She explored him with her tongue and he tightened his hold on her, halting her movements.

"I can't," he rasped. "I'm too close."

She lifted her head, satisfied that she was in his power. That she was going to do this her way.

She tore open the packet and rolled the condom onto him, then straightened and wrapped her arms around his neck, kissing him, drawing him down onto her.

"Not yet," he said, lowering his head again, kissing her breasts, her ribs, her stomach. Her breath caught when he lingered at the tender skin beneath her belly button. Then he parted her thighs gently, his tongue hot and unexpected against her core.

She arched off the bed, scrambling for something to hold on to, finding his shoulders and clinging tight. "Eduardo…"

His breath was hot on her sensitive skin, his lips hovering just above her. "Now tell me you're sorry, Hannah." Another light touch of his tongue sent a flash of brief pleasure through her.

She put one hand over her face, her cheeks burning, her body begging for release.

"Tell me, Hannah." He kissed her inner thigh and her body shook.

"No."

The tip of his tongue blazed a trail from where he'd kissed her, straight to her clitoris. Just a tease. Nothing more. "Do you want to come or not?"

"You…bastard," she panted.

He chuckled. "That doesn't sound like an apology."

"It wasn't."

He moved his hand between her thighs, his thumb sliding over her slick flesh. She gripped both his shoulders, hard, her teeth locked together. Her hips moved in rhythm with his touch. His fleeting, too-light touch.

"Touch me, dammit," she said.

"Not until you tell me you're sorry."

Her muscles were shaking, her body begging her tongue to simply say the words. She needed release. She needed him. To hell with control. "I'm sorry."

He gave her a wicked grin, then lowered his head, his tongue working magic on her as he slid one finger inside her tight body.

"Oh, yes," she breathed. It had been worth it. No amount of pride was valuable enough to hold on to, and miss this.

He lavished attention on her, fully, completely, with his mouth and hands. Something started tightening inside of her. Tension she was afraid might break her.

A second finger joined the first and the tension in her broke, shattering through her like a million glittering stars. There was no thought; there was nothing but the blinding intensity of her release.

When she returned to earth, he was there, poised above her, dark eyes intent on hers. He pushed her hair off her damp forehead, his hand shaking. Evidence that he didn't have the control he'd appeared to have. "Now," he said.

He put his hand on her thigh and lifted it so her leg hooked over his hip. The thick head of his erection pressed against her body and she arched into him. He slid in easily, filling her, stretching her in the best way.

She gripped his shoulders, her nails digging into his skin. He began to move, his thrusts hard, controlled and perfect. She moved against him, met his every move. Each time their bodies connected a sharp, white-hot sensation of pleasure struck her. She didn't think it was possible to be so turned on so quickly again.

But she was. She was craving release, needing more of the heady rush he'd always given her.

His breath was hot on her neck, quick and harsh. She turned her head and kissed his cheek, and he turned, catching her mouth, a shudder rolling through his body as she slid her tongue against his.

"*Dios,* yes," he ground out.

The controlled nature of his thrusts frayed; his movements turning choppy, desperate, keeping time with the manic need that was rolling through her, demanding release again.

He thrust into her one last time, his muscles going stiff, his entire body freezing as he found his release on a feral groan. She flexed against him and her own orgasm washed over her, waves of pleasure coursing through her as her body tightened around his. He was so deep in her, so connected with her, and in that moment, it was all that mattered.

He collapsed onto his forearms, his breathing harsh, his muscles trembling. Then he separated from her body and gathered her close to him, her backside curving into his body, his hand resting on her stomach.

They didn't speak for a long moment; the only sounds in the room were their broken, uneven breaths. He curled a lock of her hair around his finger, the touch comforting, almost as intimate as sex in a strange way.

Her brain felt foggy. Events from only moments ago running together, reduced to points of aching need and sweeping, powerful release. Sometime soon, she might feel humiliation at the fact that she'd given him so much, so quickly.

But not now.

"I didn't forget how to do it," he said finally, still out of breath.

She laughed. "What does that mean?"

"You are the first woman I've been with since my accident. I suppose I've been true to our marriage vows all this time," he said, a strange note in his voice.

It was her instinct to try and ruin the moment. To break the spell of closeness that seemed woven around them. But she couldn't. She didn't want to. She just wanted a moment. Then tomorrow, she could go back to holding him at a distance. Things could go back to the way they'd been. Mystery solved. Sexual tension broken.

But now, just now, she wouldn't ruin it.

"So have I," she said softly.

"You have what?" he asked.

"Been true to our marriage vows. I haven't…I haven't been with anyone since our wedding."

"And you didn't even know we were still married," he said.

"No. But I imagine both of us had reasons other than that for staying out of physical relationships." A stupid thing to say, because she didn't want to get into her reasons.

"There's never been time." He paused. "Or desire. I haven't truly wanted anyone since it happened. I've been too busy licking my wounds."

"And tonight you licked me," she said, injecting some completely inappropriate levity, trying to draw the topic away from where it was.

He laughed and rolled her beneath him, kissing her lips. "I have to go take care of things."

He got out of bed and she watched him walk to the bathroom. Watched the masculine, perfect shape of his backside. He was gorgeous, no question.

He returned a moment later, his expression stormy. "We have a problem."

CHAPTER EIGHT

"What?" Hannah tugged the covers up over her breasts and even with the current issue hammering away in his head, he felt a pang of regret.

"The condom broke." Something that had never happened to him before. He knew it was possible, but what the hell was the point of them if they were so fragile? "Are you on birth control?"

She hesitated. "No?"

"What's that supposed to mean? Why did you say it like you don't know?"

"I…I do know. I'm not. I mean…I didn't need to be. I mean…but things happen. These things do. The odds are so low. And I mean, a little leak will hardly…"

"Release millions of sperm?"

She cringed. "Well, okay, when you put it that way. But…"

"But it's enough to cause an accident."

Her expression turned dark. "I know how all that works, but thank you for educating me."

"I'm being realistic. We may have a situation."

"We won't," she bit out. "No one is that unlucky."

Anger boiled in his stomach. Of course it would be unlucky to be pregnant; it would be unlucky for both of them. But it struck a blow to his pride. All he could think was that she wouldn't want to be shackled to a *stupid* man for the rest of her life.

"Well," he said, his tone soft, deadly, "if you are so unlucky as to be carrying my child, be sure to let me know."

"I'll deliver the message by rock through your office window," she spat.

"Appreciated." He turned toward his room, his broad back filling the door. She'd pushed him away again. But she had to. She really had to.

It was the only way she could protect herself.

"Don't think you're going to force an apology out of me this time," she said.

He froze, his shoulders rising slightly before he turned, his eyebrows drawn together. "Don't play like I forced you, Hannah, when we both know you were begging."

She curled her fingers around the bedding. "Go away, Eduardo."

"Running again?" She opened her mouth and he cut her off. "Oh, yes, Hannah, you're running, even if you are staying in your bed. You have to do it by making a bitchy comment or whatever you think it will take to push me, or anyone else in your life, away. You don't fool me. You aren't hiding your fear from me. I will leave, only because I have no desire to spend another moment in your company tonight. But understand, you're not pushing me away if I don't want to be pushed."

He turned and walked out, shutting the door firmly behind him.

Hannah sat in the middle of the big bed, naked, physically and emotionally. She picked up one of the silken pink pillows and threw it in the direction of the closed door. It was safer to be angry than to cry again. She wasn't going to cry. She wasn't going to think about the torn condom. What that might mean.

She wasn't going to think about how it had felt to have him inside of her. Connected with her.

She really wasn't going to think about how it had been

the first time she'd felt close to someone in her entire life. And she wasn't going to think about how much she wanted to do it again.

When Hannah appeared at breakfast she didn't look much like a corporate barracuda who spat venom at unwitting victims with little warning. She looked nervous. Her blond hair was tousled and there were dark circles under her eyes. Her skinny-cut black pants and fitted, black short-sleeved shirt enhanced the thinness of her frame, and the paleness of her skin.

Eduardo leaned back in his chair and raised his coffee mug to his lips. His mother and sisters both nodded in greeting.

"Morning," Hannah said, not making eye contact with him as she took her seat at the table.

"Good morning," he said, setting his mug down on the table, taking no satisfaction in the shudder of her shoulders when his mug clattered against the glass tabletop. "Did you sleep well?"

She forced a smile. "Not really. You hogged the covers all night."

"My apologies, *querida*."

"None needed. Some coffee might be nice, though."

His mother reached out and rang a bell that sat at the center of the table. Eduardo cringed. He hated that thing. He was far too modern-minded to ring for his servants. But Carmela Vega insisted. She was old money and old class. Although, perhaps that had little to do with it, because he could easily imagine Hannah ringing for servants.

"Thank you," Hannah said to his mother.

"De nada."

Rafael came in and Hannah ordered her coffee to her specifications. She really did look exhausted. Pity he hadn't been able to keep her up all night in the way he'd like to have kept her up all night. But the fact that he'd irritated the sleep out of her was a close second as far as his personal satisfaction went.

"What are your plans for the day, Mama?" he asked.

"I thought Selena and I might go down to the shops."

Only his mother would leave Barcelona and shop in a small, seaside town. "That sounds like fun."

Selena turned her attention to Hannah. "You can join us, if you like, Hannah."

Hannah looked like a large-eyed woodland creature caught in the pull of headlights. "I...I..."

"Hannah and I have work today." He didn't want to let her out of his sight for the day. She might run. "She's helping me implement some new systems at Vega. Hannah is something of a financial genius."

"Is that right?" Carmela asked, eyebrows raised.

"I've been busy the past five years," Hannah said, her tone soft. She was so subdued. It was very unlike her and he found he didn't care for it.

"Yes, well, that is commendable," his mother said. "We'll leave you two."

"*Adiós,* Eduardo. Bye, Hannah," Selena said, standing with her mother and exiting the room.

"Your mother hates me," Hannah said when the women disappeared.

He shrugged. "Maybe."

Rafael returned with a fresh cup of coffee and a half-filled French press. *"Gracias,"* Hannah said, taking a sip of her already-prepared coffee. Rafael left again and Hannah set her mug down. "I would rather if she didn't hate me, but I suppose it doesn't do any good for her to like me since I'm leaving again...whenever. As soon as we get these systems in place and you feel comfortable."

"I suppose not." He found his body rebelled at the idea of her leaving. He felt possessive of her now. Stupid because before his accident he'd slept with any number of women and he'd never felt possessive of them. Quite the opposite, he'd felt ready to bolt out of bed, call them a cab and see they were safely delivered home so that he could sleep. Alone.

He frowned. The memories pricked his conscience and he realized that he didn't like the way he'd treated women then. He wondered if that had to do with the accident, with the changes in him, or just being older.

Interesting, since he normally envied the man he'd once been to a certain extent. But not in that area. He'd been a playboy, happily seeking release with any willing woman. Now the emptiness of that echoed in him.

With Hannah it had been more. More than release. More than amusement. It had been something serious, something that made him feel different in the bright light of day. He was angry with her, for the way she'd acted after, and still, he felt a connection with her that hadn't been there before.

As if, when he'd parted from her last night, he'd left a piece of himself behind.

"What is the work plan for the day?" she asked, her expression projecting extreme annoyance and boredom at the same time.

"Bring your coffee up to my office."

She stood and waited for him, then followed him out of the room and up the curving staircase, down to the end of the hall. His home office faced the sea, large expansive windows letting in plenty of natural light. And all easily covered with blinds that dropped at the push of a button. Just in case he got hit with a particularly bad migraine.

Fortunately, he felt fine. Which meant the only headache he would have to contend with was Hannah.

"Did you have anything more to show me?" she asked.

"No. I was hoping you would start presenting some solutions."

She shifted her weight to the balls of her feet. She looked like she was ready to sprint away if need be. "Actually, I do have some solutions. Well, thoughts mainly."

"Do you?"

"Yes. You prefer to work here now?"

"It's noisy in the office. I don't care for it."

"Right, which is why you have your floor essentially vacant," she said slowly.

"Yes. I can't handle the noise of all the people talking all the time. Even without people working on the floor, the interruptions, the traffic, it can start to…"

"It wears on you."

An understatement. The lowest moment in his memory was of throwing a mug at the wall in front of his secretary when she'd come in talking and he'd been in the throes of a migraine. It hadn't been aimed at her, and it hadn't come anywhere near her, but the blinding pain and anger…the fact he'd had no control over it in that moment. That he'd frightened her. It lived with him.

She'd quit soon after and he couldn't blame her.

"I find things easier here," he said, looking at his hands.

Hannah frowned. "Did you have trouble working around people before?"

"I just don't like noise," he said.

"What about it?"

He looked out at the sea, frowning. He'd been through some of this with a doctor years ago, and had since given up. He didn't like talking about how nothing had changed. There was no point. "It makes my head hurt."

"Anything else?"

"And I get irritable."

"Yeah, I've noticed," she said dryly. "What else?"

"I can't concentrate," he bit out.

"And numbers, finances, they give you the most trouble."

"I can't…I can't hang on to a thought about it for long enough to make decisions."

"And it's high pressure," she said, pushing.

"Yes."

"I think it might have less to do with you having trouble understanding the financial side of things and more to do with you having a harder time focusing on things that stress you out."

An uncomfortable tightness invaded his stomach. "It does not stress me out. I just… The answers are there in my brain but I can't seem to make a fast decision. I can't find the answer in time. Or at all." And the more he thought about it, the less able he was to reach out and grasp onto a thought firmly. It slipped away from him, hiding deep in the dark corners of his brain that seemed unknowable to him now.

"It does stress you out. Why haven't you talked to a doctor about this? I'm sure…"

"I don't need to talk to a doctor," he said, something exploding inside of him. "Not again. I don't need to go and sit there, and outline the same problems and have some old man look at me with pity in his eyes as he tells me, again, that they may never go away. That I will never be the man I was. That I won't have all the answers, or a witty joke on hand. That I will never be able to take the reins of Vega as I should have been able to, because I will never be able to make snap decisions, or keep meticulous records."

He planted his hands on his desk and leaned in so that his face was a breath from hers. "I can't concentrate long enough to fill out a damn report. How am I supposed to keep track of intricate financial details? Do you know the answer?" He pushed off and straightened, running his hand through his hair. "Do you?" he asked again, his voice sounding rougher this time, desperate. He loathed it. Despised himself in that moment. He was shaking. With anger. Fear.

"I…I just don't know," she said softly. "But we can figure it out."

He swallowed hard, his chest seizing up tight. "Or maybe I should just concede to the fact that I can't."

She stood and slapped her palms down on his desk before

rounding to the front, her blue eyes blazing. "No. That's…
that's just wrong, Eduardo. You can do this. You aren't stupid. What I said…that was wrong, too. And I'll apologize
for that willingly, with no…coercion." Her face turned pink
when she said that last part. "It's just a matter of figuring out
loopholes. Shortcuts."

Anger burned in him. At her. At the world. "I shouldn't
need them," he growled.

"But we all do sometimes," she said, her tone rising with
his.

"Maybe you do, Hannah Weston, but I don't. I am Eduardo
Vega, son of one of the greatest business minds that ever
lived, and I sure as hell should not need a shortcut."

"Then it's your pride keeping you from succeeding. Not
your injury. Keep that in mind if you start losing a handle
on things again. I can't help you if you won't accept help."

"I am accepting help," he shouted, well beyond his limits
now. Beyond the point of sublimating his rage. "Why do you
think I asked you here?"

Hannah came closer, not cowed by his outburst. "You
didn't ask me here. You all but forced me and you know it.
And you aren't accepting help. Did you think I would come in,
take a look at things, make some investments and leave you?"

"Yes," he said, realizing as he spoke the word that it was
true.

"Just leave you without solving the problem?"

"Yes," he said again. Because he hadn't wanted to admit
there was a real problem. A reset. He'd been after a reset. To
get everything back to a golden point so he could move forward, steering the ship, on course again.

That he would see Hannah, and remember who he was.
Not just remember, but feel those same feelings. That amusement, that desire and ability to simply flip his middle finger
at the world, enjoying his position of success, feeling invincible. Untouchable.

Far from that, he felt like he was drowning, reaching blindly for a hand. Hannah's hand. Praying she would be able to hold him above water.

Such weakness. Such horrifying, unendurable weakness.

"That can't happen, Eduardo," she said.

"Why not?" he asked, drained now, the anger, the fight, leaving him in a rush. Leaving him defeated.

He looked so bleak. Hannah had never seen that expression on his face before. Had never seen him look so tired. And in spite of the fact that she'd been determined to hang on to anger where he was concerned, she found in that moment she couldn't.

It had been easy to fight him, to rage at him while he was raging at her. But she saw beneath it now. Saw it for what it was.

"Because things have changed. You've changed." She wasn't telling him anything he didn't know. But she wondered if she was the first person, other than doctors, who'd been brave enough to tell the almighty Eduardo Vega the real and absolute truth he didn't want to hear. "And all you can do is work with what you have. Not what you wish you had, not what you once had, but what you have, here and now."

He shook his head. "I don't want to." It didn't sound petulant like it might have, it simply sounded dry. Resigned.

"Eduardo, you were always fun in your way. A bit of an ass, I mean, enough of one that you blackmailed me into marrying you as a way to goad your father. But you were easygoing, outgoing. And you never would have taken the responsibility of running Vega seriously. You used to kill me with your smug smile and your dismissal of your duties. Everything was a game to you. And now…now it's not. Now I believe you have it in you to do it. So yeah, maybe there are some other issues, but you can work around those. We can work around those."

He let out a slow, shaking breath. "So I am forced to confront the fact that I would never have chosen to live up to my full potential before, and now that I would…now that I would, my potential is greatly diminished."

"That's not it at all." Her stomach tightened, that fierce feeling of empathy, of connection, she'd felt with him that day his mother had arrived at the house intensified. Until that moment she hadn't felt closer to him since they'd slept together. If anything, she'd felt like any connection they might have had had been severed. But now it was back, and it was stronger.

He laughed. "It's not? Enlighten me then, Hannah."

"It will only be that if you insist on beating your head against a brick wall you could walk around if you weren't so stubborn. If you weren't letting your pride have control."

He raised his head, dark eyes glittering. "Pride is the one thing I still have."

She shook her head. "It's not. Trust me."

"It's myself I don't trust," he said, his eyes blank. "I don't know my own mind."

"Then learn it. When you're ready." She walked past him and out the door of the office. She was feeling…too much. Feeling in general. Tomorrow they would go back to Barcelona. She could get back to the business of seeing him as business. She could forget that this weekend ever happened.

She had to.

CHAPTER NINE

EDUARDO drew a hand over his face, fighting the anger, the frustration that was mounting inside of him. Then he gave up, giving it free rein as he pushed every piece of paper off his desk in a broad sweep and watched them all flutter to the floor.

He took a sharp breath, trying to gain a hold on himself. Trying to satisfy the dark, uncontrollable feelings that were firing through his veins. He put his head down and pushed his fingers through his hair, trying, desperately to think of what he'd just read.

Nothing. There was nothing. A void. A blank void that the information had fallen into and no matter how hard he tried, he couldn't get it back.

He let out a growl of frustration and picked his paper-weight up from his desk, hurling it at the wall. Not even that helped. Nothing helped.

He pushed back from his desk and put his hands on his head as he paced.

The door to his office opened and Hannah walked in, the corners of her lips turned down. "Are you okay?"

Something in him shifted when he saw Hannah. It had been three weeks since they'd been back from his ranch. Three weeks of living together like strangers. Of pretending they'd never touched each other. That he'd never been inside her.

It was slowly driving him crazy. The financial reports from his retail stores were finishing the job. Quickly.

"Do I look okay?" he asked, moving his hand in a broad stroke in front of him, indicating the papers on the floor.

"No," she said, closing the door behind her. "What's up?"

"I can't do it, Hannah." The words burned his throat. "I can't remember. I can't..."

"Hey, take a breath."

"I did take a breath," he said through clenched teeth. "Then I realized it didn't fix anything so I destroyed my office instead."

"Productive."

In spite of himself, he snorted a laugh. "I thought so. Just as productive as me attempting to comprehend anything in these reports."

"Eduardo..."

He turned away from her, from the pained expression in her eyes and looked out at the city. "Do you have any idea how...frustrating it is, to have such a lack of control. To... I can't make it work. I can't make my mind what it was. I can't make it what I want." A dagger of pain pierced his temple and he winced.

"Maybe you should take a break."

He turned back to her. "I don't have time for a break."

"Then maybe ask for help instead of being so stubborn!"

The anger drained from him, as sudden and as uncontrollable as it had come on. And now he just felt exhausted. Down to his bones. "Help me, Hannah."

Something in her expression softened. If she tried to touch him...if she said she was sorry...he couldn't handle that.

Then, just as suddenly as the softness had appeared, it was replaced by her mask of hard efficiency. A mask he needed her to wear.

"What do you need help with?"

"In general. Help. All the help you can give me. I can't

focus on this." He indicated the papers again. "I can't retain it. I can barely read it. The words just keep…moving. I don't know why. Today it's like everything is moving too fast. I can't…"

She bent and gathered up the papers, glancing at the page numbers and, with a speed that made him vaguely jealous, put them in order.

"Close your eyes." He frowned. "Do it," she said.

He complied and felt a rush of calm go through him. All of the light and busy surroundings shut out, and he felt like he could think a bit better.

She started reading. Out loud. To him. Like he was a child who needed a bedtime story. About the amount of returns over the Christmas shopping season.

He straightened in his chair, his eyes popping open. "I'm not a child."

"I know. I'm not treating you like one. What I'm curious to know is how it is for you to listen to things rather than read them. Some people are auditory learners rather than visual."

"I never had a problem with visual…"

"Before. I know. But that was before."

"How do you know so much about this?"

"About learning? I had to teach myself how to learn when I decided I wanted to go to college. So, I researched every studying trick imaginable. Every way I could think of to do well on tests. I had to take an entrance exam, you know? And I only went to two years of high school. I had to study more than anyone else going into those tests, and I wasn't a natural intellectual. But I needed to be. So I learned to be."

"What kinds of things did you do?"

"Well, sometimes I would record my notes, and then play them back in headphones before going to sleep. I would write things out dozens of times. Drink coffee while I was study-ing, and again while I was taking the test. Taste is a really powerful memory trigger it turns out. Anyway, I don't see why we can't try to apply the principles to you."

A strange feeling moved through him. Respect? Yes, respect for Hannah. Intense and strong. And with that, the feelings of attraction he'd been working so hard to repress over the past few weeks.

Every time he'd passed her as she went into her office on his otherwise secluded floor. Every time he passed her in the hall in his home. Every time he closed his eyes at night and thought of her, so near, and yet so unobtainable.

"You are very clever, Hannah. Smart."

"No less for needing to use those tricks?"

"More so, perhaps. You found ways to make it work for you."

"And that's what you'll do, Eduardo." She lifted the stack of papers again. "Now, close your eyes."

This time he let her read and he found he had an easier time grasping meaning. Holding on to details that had passed through his mind before like water through a sieve. And when she quizzed him at the end, he could remember most of what he'd heard. Not all, but much more than he would have remembered had he read through it, and in much less time.

Now, when he spoke to his managers he wouldn't sound completely ignorant. Would sound more like a man who was equipped to hold his position.

"Better," he said, rising from his chair and rounding the desk.

"Yes," she agreed, a smile on her beautiful face. Was she happy for him? Or was it her own success that had her beaming from ear to ear in such an uncharacteristic way? "Now this is an easy one. You just need phone calls. They can fax you the reports so you can have them on file, but you can get a verbal briefing on the phone."

"You are truly a genius, Hannah," he said. And impulsively, he leaned forward and kissed her on the cheek. "Thank you."

She put her hand up to her cheek, her eyes round. "You're welcome."

He realized it was the first time he'd touched her since their night together. Unbidden, images of her hands on his body, his mouth on her breasts, came into his mind. He'd been without sex for five years until recently, largely of his own accord, and now three weeks without seemed a hellish eternity.

"Hannah…"

She backed away. "No. Not… I'm glad that that's helping. I want to keep helping. I'm really close to being able to give you some nice projected stats on how well we could do if we bought out Bach Wireless. But…no."

He hadn't realized that the hunger inside of him had been projected so clearly. And of course she'd said no. Of course she had. She should. Being with her had been like being thrown into a fire. It had been all-consuming, a flame that would ravage and devour everything in its path. He didn't have the kind of time needed to devote to something like that.

He had to focus on Vega. He had to keep things moving forward. They both needed to be fully engaged in business for that. Not fully engaged in bedroom games.

"Back to work then," he said.

She nodded curtly and walked out of the room. He tried to ignore the ache that started in his groin and seemed to spread to his entire body. Hannah was off-limits. If he said it enough times, he might start to believe it.

She was late. She was late, late, late. And her shady, private detour was making her late for work, and not just for her period. She wanted to crawl under the potted plant in the lobby of Vega Communications and cry. But she didn't have time.

She had to go pee on a stick, see one line instead of two, and get to work.

Eduardo was already in his office on the top floor. She walked past, trying to keep her steps quick but quiet, trying to keep from disturbing him as she made her way to the private bathroom at the end of the floor. She closed herself in and locked it, unwrapping the box that contained the test with shaking fingers.

The test itself was wrapped in some sort of heinous, indestructible foil. Keys. She did have the keys from home in her purse. She grabbed one and jabbed at the packaging until she worked the slim, innocuous-looking white test free.

Actually taking the test was easy. It was the wait that was hard.

She'd never imagined she'd be back in this position again. Except, instead of huddling in a cramped, filthy bathroom in her childhood home, shaking and on the verge of vomiting, she was huddled in a gorgeous, spotlessly clean bathroom on the highest floor of one of the world's largest and most prestigious companies. Shaking and on the verge of vomiting.

She paced while she waited. And counted. And closed her eyes. And considered throwing up.

"Just one," she whispered. "Just one line." She opened her eyes slowly and looked down at the white test lying on the white counter. All that stark white made it impossible to miss the two glaring pink lines that had bled into the test.

And then she did throw up.

"Hannah?" The door behind her shook as Eduardo knocked on it heavily. "Are you okay? Are you sick?"

"Yes," she called back. She shifted so that she was sitting inelegantly by the toilet, a cold sweat had broken out across her forehead, down her back.

"You're okay or you're sick?"

"I'm sick," she called back.

"Do you need help?"

"No." She pulled into a sitting position and took the test

off the counter, wrapping it four times over in toilet paper before throwing it into the garbage.

Why was this happening to her? Why was she being punished for sex? Was she just extremely fertile? Or extremely unlucky.

Everything started hitting her. The test she'd taken at sixteen. All the options she'd weighed then. Going to the clinic. Leaving the clinic, on a dead run, unable to go through with ending the pregnancy. Going to the adoption agency. The first time she'd felt the baby move. How strange, miraculous and heartbreaking it had been.

Labor and delivery. That brief flash of pink, wrinkled skin. Her baby squalling as he was taken from the room and to his parents.

He wasn't her baby. He belonged to Steve and Carol Johnson. He was their son. But he still felt like part of her. Part of her she couldn't get back. Part of her she'd had to give up. And with him, she gave up so much more.

And then she'd made a promise. That she would do everything to be the best she could be. That she wouldn't waste her life. Through extreme pain, physically and emotionally, she'd been given a wake-up call and she had vowed she would make the absolute most of it.

And she had. She'd done it. She'd made a success of herself. She'd let go of the girl she'd been. At least she thought she had. She didn't feel like it now. She just felt scared.

She couldn't do it again. She couldn't. It would break her.

Loss, a deep, unending sense of loss filled her and she put her hands on her stomach to try and stop the pain from spreading.

"Hannah? Do I have to break the door in?"

She shook off the pain, tried to find her strength. Tried to find Hannah Weston, so she wouldn't drown in Hannah Hackett. "You'll do yourself another head injury, Ed, so maybe don't."

"Hannah," he growled.

She turned on the sink and ran cold water over her hands, dragging them over her face, not caring if she smeared her makeup. Then she jerked the door open and came face-to-face with Eduardo. She had no idea what to say to him.

"Hi."

"You look terrible," he said.

"Thanks"

"You're pale," he said. "And you look like...well, you look sick."

"I am," she snapped.

"Do you need anything?"

A time machine. So she could go back to four weeks earlier when she'd decided having sex with him would be a way to regain control. It hadn't worked. Not in the least. And it certainly wasn't worth the consequence.

"I don't think there's anything you could do for me at the moment. Let's go in your office."

One thing she wasn't, was a coward. She wasn't going to hide it from him. It was implausible at best. So she would tell him. But she didn't know what she would tell him. She was the world's worst candidate to be a mother. But she honestly didn't know if she could go through giving up another child.

But she wasn't sure if she could be a mother, either. She knew nothing about it. She'd never had one. She didn't know if she had a nurturing bone in her body. She was insensitive. She swore. She was a workaholic. She had a criminal history.

The list went on.

"Sit down," she said.

"Hannah, what is it?"

"You remember how we had sex?"

One of his dark eyebrows shot up. "Yes, I seem to remember something about that."

"Right, well...also, remember the condom broke."

"I do remember," he said, his tone turning heavy, wooden.

"Well, I…we…that is…you…"

"You're pregnant."

"Well, when you say it like that you make it sound like it's all my fault. But you know I didn't get that way on my own."

"Hannah, I am well aware of how it happened and I am not fobbing the blame off onto you, so stop panicking for a second," he growled.

"Stop? Stop panicking? Eduardo, I have barely started panicking. There is an entire repertoire of panic for me to work through before I can even begin to wind down the panicking."

"There's no need to panic."

"Why is there no need to panic?"

"Because we're more than capable of handling this situation."

"Are we?" she asked, her throat almost completely constricted. "Do you have any idea… I mean. Do you? And what will we do with a baby, Eduardo, what? Will you strap him to your chest and bring him to work? You can't concentrate as it is. And me…what? I'm going to put on an apron and turn into Susie Homemaker?"

"We'll get nannies," he said.

"What kind of life is that for a child?"

"A life. There doesn't seem to be an alternative."

"Adoption," she said. The word sounded flat and cold in the room.

"I'm not giving away my child."

His words hurt. They cut her deep, tapped into a wound still raw and bleeding, covered, but never healed. "That's not what adoption is. It's giving your child the best chance possible. That's what it is. Wouldn't…wouldn't I have been better off? If my mother had given me up instead of neglecting me for three years of my life and then dropping me off with a father who didn't want me?" She couldn't voice the rest. Couldn't say anything about how this had happened before. It all just stuck in her throat. Painful. Horrendous. "Do you understand what it's like? To live with someone who just doesn't give a damn about what you do? Who doesn't even worry about you if you stay out all night? I was doing everything you should be afraid your child is out doing. Drinking, and having sex and he never... He didn't care. So tell me, Eduardo, what kind of life was that? Why should a child, anyone, ever live where they aren't wanted?"

"Are you saying you don't want the baby?"

"No. That's not it...that's not..."

"We could take care of a child, Hannah. It's different. We both have money."

"Money isn't enough."

"It's a start, at least."

She took a shaky breath. "Nothing has to be decided now," she said finally. "It's early. There's no need to—" she laughed "—well, to panic."

Eduardo felt like he'd been hit in the chest. He couldn't breathe. He could hardly think. Hannah was pregnant. The only time he'd ever thought about children had been in terms of preventing them. He'd vaguely assumed, prior to his injury, that he would settle down for real one day and in that scenario, there had been a hazy assumption of children, but he'd never truly thought about it in a real sense.

And since his accident...well, he'd avoided women. Avoided all kinds of relationships. The thought of having a child when everything was so much harder than it had once been... Hannah was right in many ways. He wasn't sure he could handle being a father and running Vega. He could scarcely run Vega, and Hannah knew it better than most.

Knew what sorts of limitations she was dealing with when it came to the father of her baby.

"Right," he said, as if having decided that maybe they could just put it out of their minds for a while, but he doubted he would think of anything else. He wasn't sure how he ever could.

"Right," she said, looking as unconvinced as he felt.

"Let's go back to the *rancho*," he said. He needed solitude. Quiet. He needed to not be here, in this place that reminded him of his shortcomings.

"What? When?"

"This weekend," he said. "I don't think I can…concentrate here. There's too much. This…makes it too much."

"Right," she said. "I just need my phone glued to me because I have to get that deal nailed down."

"I understand. We'll bring work with us." But the room felt like it was closing in on him, the whole city, just outside the windows, felt like it was folding on top of him. His mind was cluttered and he couldn't figure out how to sift through it. Especially not with the pounding that was starting in his head. With the way the light was starting to feel, like a knife going in through his eyes.

"We leave tomorrow."

Hannah nodded, for once without any kind of sassy comeback. "Okay."

CHAPTER TEN

"ARE you all right staying in here?"

Hannah looked around the frilly pink-and-white room. The room she and Eduardo had made love in. The room they'd conceived the baby in.

"As fine here as I would be anywhere," she said, her head spinning, a strange, heavy numbness invading her chest and spreading outward. She was so tired. Exhaustion seeped into her bones.

"I want to be close to you."

"I'm not going to do anything desperate, Eduardo."

"I know."

Except he didn't know. And that was fair enough, because she'd never really let him know her. He'd seen her naked and he still didn't know her. No one did. Not really. She wasn't sure she did anymore. Wasn't sure what she wanted. Wasn't sure if she could clear the next hurdle that had been placed in front of her.

Just the thought of what the next few months would bring, of what it would mean to watch her baby be carried from the room again, never holding him, never touching him, made her feel cold. Made her feel like the life was draining from her.

What if you kept him?

For a moment she imagined it. Holding her baby at her breast, looking into eyes that were dark like his father's. Having someone to love. Someone who would love her.

Her stomach seized, tears threatening to fall.

"I'm fine," she said, mostly for her own benefit. But she knew she was lying.

"Do you want to lie down for a while?"

"I'm not symptomatic yet."

"When does that usually start?"

"Six weeks or so," she said.

He frowned. "Do all women just…know this stuff? You don't seem like you would."

Shoot. Yes, she would have to tell him sometime. It wasn't like it would matter. Except it did. It was her pain. It had never been anyone else's.

"You'd be surprised," she said. "I am a little tired. I think I'll take a nap. We'll talk later?"

He nodded curtly. "If you feel up to it, I'd like to walk down to the beach with you."

"That would be great."

She ushered him out of the room and rested her back against the closed door. Her old life was crashing head-on into her new one, and she wasn't sure anymore where one ended and the other began.

It was her worst nightmare unfolding in front of her. And she wasn't sure there was anything she could do to stop it.

She woke up feeling sleepier than she had when she'd lain down. Her head was swimming, and it was dark outside. So she'd missed her walk. It was okay, though; she hadn't really felt up to talking to Eduardo. Not now. Not when she'd have to be honest with him.

A tear rolled down her face and back into her hair and she didn't bother to wipe it away. Eduardo was the only person she'd felt close to in so long, and even they were in opposition half the time.

Maybe she wasn't meant to be close to people. It was pretty obvious she didn't really know how to be. Even with Zack there had been calculated distance. They hadn't shared themselves. They'd met where they were at in life and moved forward, never digging deep, never really getting to know each other. And she'd been happy with that.

Eduardo pushed her; he made her angry. Made her feel passion and lose control. It didn't make her all that happy, and it had led to a pretty big mistake. But she did feel more genuine when she was with him. More herself.

She wasn't sure if that was a good thing or not.

She pulled her knees up to her chest and rolled to her side. She felt like she was breaking apart. For once she couldn't outthink a situation. Couldn't control it or change it. It was what it was. She was pregnant. With Eduardo's baby.

She sat up and wiped the tears from her cheeks. She needed to get her mind off it. She needed to be near Eduardo, and she couldn't fathom why. But it didn't matter why. She hurt everywhere. She felt like she was being scraped raw inside.

And she was so tired of being alone. She was always alone.

With shaking limbs she stood from the bed and padded across the room, to the door that separated her room from Eduardo's, walking into his room without knocking.

For a moment, she didn't see him. It was dark in his room, and he wasn't in the bed. Then she saw him, slumped in his chair, his hands gripping the armrests.

"Hi," she said, her voice sounding huskier than she intended it to.

He shifted. "Hannah? Are you feeling all right?"

"As well as can be expected. Yourself?"

"I had a migraine. I'm better now."

"Have you been drinking?"

"No. That makes it worse. Why?"

"Just…it's good to know. I…I really need you," she whispered.

"What?"

"I can't be alone. And I'm cold. I need you to make me

feel…make me feel again." She battled against the tears that were threatening to fall, threatening to choke her. "Make me warm."

He stood quickly and wrapped his arm around her waist, pulling her up against him. "Hannah…"

"I just want to stop thinking. For a minute. I just want to feel. You make me feel so good. When you touch me…" She swallowed hard. "I'm asking you for help now, Eduardo."

"Oh, Hannah."

He picked her up, holding her close to his chest, and she wrapped her arms around his neck. She'd never given a lot of thought to her feelings on over-the-top masculine displays of strength. Turned out, she liked them.

She placed her palms flat over his chest, over the hard muscles, maddeningly concealed by his thin T-shirt. She lowered her hands and found the hem of the shirt, sliding her fingertips up his hot, hair-roughened skin.

He groaned and set her down on the bed, tugging the shirt over his head. She could see the outline of his body, moonlight gleaming from the hard ridges of his chest and abs, his jeans low cut, delicious lines pointing right down to his erection.

And that was all she was going to think about. Just him.

"You're really sexy," she breathed.

He chuckled, his hands on his belt buckle. "So are you. Trade."

She tugged her shirt over her head and lay back, waiting for the rest of Eduardo to be revealed.

He shook his head. "Not enough."

"Grr." She got up on her knees and torqued her arms around, unhooking her bra and sending it sailing. "Better?"

The heat glittering in his dark eyes sent an answering fire down to her belly. And farther down.

A smile curved his lips. "Much better."

He worked his belt through the loops and tugged it free.

Then shrugged off his pants and underwear in one deft motion.

"Come here," she said.

"Your wish is my command."

He joined her on the bed, his bare shaft hot against her stomach. "Oh, yes," she whispered, the edges of her mind getting fuzzy with arousal. This was what she needed.

He unbuttoned her jeans and tugged them down her legs, then quickly took her underwear down with them. He teased her with his fingers, his thumb sliding over her clitoris.

She arched into him, clawing at his back, letting her mind go blank of everything but the white-hot pleasure that was pouring through her.

Then he bracketed her face with his hands, kissing her. Deep. Long. Passionate. She clung to him, letting the kiss intensify, learning his rhythm, relearning her own.

This was less intimate than the way he'd touched her a moment ago, but also, somehow, infinitely more so. When he finally released her mouth to trail kisses down her neck, she was shaking, more turned on than she'd ever been in her life. On the verge of tears.

She forked her fingers through his hair, craving deeper contact, craving more.

He kissed her belly, heading lower.

"No," she breathed. "No time."

She needed him inside of her. As deep as he could be, as close as he could be. She hadn't needed anyone in longer than she could remember. She'd never been able to afford to.

"I need you," she said. Meaning it, with every fiber of her being. He continued down, a low chuckle escaping his lips. "No," she said. "This isn't…a game or anything. I need you."

He raised his head, moving back up her body, his dark eyes intense, locked with hers. He pushed her hair back from her face, then kissed her lightly on her lips. She parted her thighs and felt him at the entrance of her body.

"Yes," she whispered.

He slid slowly inside of her. With every inch she felt some of her emptiness fade, and when he was inside her completely, as close to her as two people could be, she felt like she understood sex in a new way entirely.

Sex had never been intimate for her. And she hadn't been after intimacy tonight. Back in high school she'd been after oblivion, a moment of happiness, of closeness even. But not true, deep intimacy.

But she felt it now. As if Eduardo had become a part of her. As if she would leave his bed changed.

He moved inside of her, every stroke perfection, driving her closer to the edge of bliss. Every thrust bringing him closer to her.

His pace increased and she locked her legs around his hips, moving with him; she arched back, her release crashing over her like a wave. He gripped the sheet by her head and shuddered out his own orgasm a moment later.

She lay against his chest, her heart pounding hard, her head swimming. She wanted to speak; she couldn't. A moment later she realized she was shaking. And crying, tears falling on his bare skin.

"I..." she started.

But there was nothing to say. She was overwhelmed. She was pregnant with this man's baby. This man who held her so tightly. Who made her feel close to someone for the first time ever.

No one had ever loved her. And she had never thought of it before. But now...now, in his arms, she wished so much that it could be different. That she could be different. That she could be loved.

He kept his arms wrapped tightly around her and held her close. She kept shaking and he reached down to grab the covers, drawing them up over both of them.

"Sleep now, *querida*. We'll talk more tomorrow."

She nodded wordlessly, unable to speak around the lump in her throat.

She curled up against him, inhaled the scent of him, so uniquely Eduardo. Then she closed her eyes and tried to fall asleep. Trying to fight off all of the demons that were threatening to tear her apart.

Eduardo woke up as the first rays of sun began to filter through the expansive windows of the room. He'd forgotten to close the blinds because his headache had hit after dark.

He rolled over to look at Hannah and his heart seized.

She was so beautiful. And achingly vulnerable. He didn't know how he'd missed it for so long. He'd imagined her invincible, a fair target to bring into his sphere. She could handle herself, after all, and he would never leave her empty-handed.

But he could see now that he'd been wrong. Very wrong.

He thought about what she'd said the day before. About him barely being able to run his business, much less run it with a baby around to distract him. She was right. And yet, when he thought back to his own childhood, the way his father had been, stern and distant, but steady and so very present, he couldn't imagine being anything less for his own child.

He had the resources to care for a son or daughter. And his mother would be thrilled.

And if you can't do it? If the crying gives you migraines and lack of sleep makes it impossible for you to concentrate? If it gets so bad you can't see? What will you do then?

He would figure it out. He had no other choice. They could get nannies, the best available. He would have to. But he could make it work.

He knew it now, with certainty. It had been too hard to process in his office, beneath the bright fluorescent lights. But now, in the gray light of dawn, with Hannah warm and naked by his side, it did seem clear.

He'd wanted to decide what to do about the baby before

anything else happened between them…but when she'd come to him, so vulnerable, so achingly sad, he hadn't been able to deny her. Especially as her misery seemed to be a reflection of his own.

She'd asked him to make her warm. She'd made him warm.

He moved his hand down to Hannah's stomach and his heart pounded faster. Harder.

"Are you awake?" he whispered.

Hannah's eyes opened slowly. "Oh…"

"You sound disappointed," he said.

She rolled over and buried her face in her pillow. "I slept with you again."

"I remember."

She rolled over again. "It wasn't a good idea. It…confuses things."

"Can things be any more confusing?"

"Oh, I don't know, but this can't possibly help clear it up."

"Okay, that's probably true." He moved into a sitting position, unconcerned with the fact that he was still naked. Hannah averted her eyes, clearly of a different opinion, clutching the sheets to her chest. "I'd like to talk to you. About the baby."

"I…" She bit her lip. "Now?"

"Why don't you go shower. I'll shower. We'll have breakfast. Then I'd like to walk with you for a while. On the beach."

She nodded slowly. "I can do that."

"Good." He leaned in and kissed her forehead, the move not planned. And he found he didn't regret it.

He got out of bed and walked toward his bathroom, taking a small amount of satisfaction in Hannah's muffled squeak, likely brought on by his continued nudity. He turned and saw her scrambling out of bed with the sheet still wrapped tightly around her body.

"You might as well let it drop, Hannah. I've seen it all."

Something in her expression changed, a sad smile lifting the corner of her lips. "Not in daylight. I'll see you in a bit."

She turned, still covered, and walked out of the room.

Hannah was done showering before Eduardo, and had a few moments down in the breakfast area by herself. She nibbled on a bowl of fruit for a while, then asked one of Eduardo's staff if she could get some bacon. Bacon sounded good. It wasn't a pregnant craving, she was pretty sure it was too soon for that. She was just feeling horrible and trying to comfort herself with food.

She nibbled on the bacon while she thought about how today would play out. Yet again, it seemed impossible to plan.

She would have to tell Eduardo. There was really no way around it. Because she had to explain to him where she was coming from.

He appeared a few moments later, dressed in shorts and sandals, ready for a casual walk on the beach. She only had one pair of jeans, so she was going to have to settle for rolling them up past her ankles.

"I'm not really hungry," he said. "Are you ready?"

She picked up another bacon strip. "Yeah." She stood and took a deep breath, following him out the back door of the house. There was a little path that cut through the meadow and led down the hillside, tall grass rising up, making the walkway feel enclosed. Private.

The ground softened and turned from dirt to sand, the chilly, salty air stinging her cheeks. They were quiet until they reached the shore.

"How are you feeling now, Hannah?"

"Now that I've had a full twenty-four hours to process it?" she asked.

"Yes."

"Not great."

"Tell me," he said, still walking. Heading toward a grove

of trees that was at the far end of the beach. "Do you still want to give the baby up?"

Her throat tightened. "It's not a matter of want, Eduardo. It's about…about doing what's best for the baby. I wasn't very nice yesterday, to you, when I said that about caring for a baby and the company, but my point is still solid. I'm married to my work, and you're willing to do anything for your job. So when exactly are we going to find the time to raise a child? And with me in the U.S. and you here in Spain…"

"So, be here."

"Me? Move to Spain?"

"You've lived here before. You liked it."

She'd more than liked it. She loved Spain. In so many ways it felt like her home. "Yes," she said slowly, "but I have a job back in San Francisco, assuming they haven't cleaned out my desk."

"You've left plenty of jobs."

"That's not really the issue."

"Then what is?"

The truth hovered on the edge of her lips, but she couldn't quite bring herself to say it, not just yet.

"My father was very much committed to his business," Eduardo said. "He was still a good father."

"You were angry with him half the time."

"I know. Because I was young and stupid and entitled. And if there's one change I am thankful for in myself, it's that my fall seems to have knocked some of the jackass out of me."

She laughed. "Some, maybe. But you still have plenty."

They reached the little cluster of trees and they walked beneath them. Hannah looked up at the green leaves, a spiderweb of sunlight breaching the foliage.

"Do you know how all-consuming a baby will be?" she asked, her stomach churning.

"I'm not sure that I do. But no parent really does until they have one of their own."

It had been years since she'd thought of that long-ago baby as her son. She couldn't. Couldn't let herself have that connection to him. Because she knew better than most that it took more than blood to be a parent. For her son, his parents were the people who had raised him. Who had stayed up nights with him. She had simply carried him.

If only that were enough to abolish the connection she felt.

"I'm afraid," she whispered, tears clogging her throat.

"Of course you are, Hannah. Childbirth is…an unknown experience. Pregnancy is certainly…"

"No." She shook her head, trying to ignore the pain that was crawling through her veins. "I know all about being pregnant. About what it's like to feel your baby move inside you for the first time… It's…it's a miracle, Eduardo." She felt a tear slide down her cheek. "Labor is as awful as they say. But in the end there's this perfect little…life. And it's so worth it. All of it. The morning sickness, the stretch marks. The pain."

"Hannah," he said, his tone flat, cold.

"I was sixteen when I got pregnant," she said. She'd never voiced the words out loud before. Had never confided in anyone. "And I knew there was no way I could take care of a baby." Another tear fell and she didn't wipe it away.

"I gave him up. Because it was the right thing to do. But… but I'm not sure I can go through it again. I don't think I could give this one up, even if I should. And I'm afraid…I'm afraid that if I do keep this baby, I'll really understand what I gave up then."

CHAPTER ELEVEN

HANNAH felt emotion coming in thick, unendurable waves. She could drown in it, in the pain, the misery. The starkness of the truth. It was so very ugly, and yet, it was a part of her.

"Hannah that must have been…"

"There are days when I'm so glad that I did it. Because I was this poor, high school dropout with no future and what could I offer him? Nothing. Nothing but more of the same. More poverty. More…neglect maybe while I tried to work and earn enough money to keep us in whatever filthy apartment I could afford. Was I going to take him back to the single-wide I shared with my dad? Expose him to secondhand smoke and mice and bugs and everything else we had to contend with?" She looked down. "But some people make it. I just…I knew I wasn't strong enough. I knew I didn't know how."

"What about the father?"

She shook her head, a faint feeling of embarrassment creeping over her, joining the misery. "I didn't really know him. He was this senior guy I hooked up with at a party. He wasn't my boyfriend. Obviously, I was very irresponsible. It wasn't the first time I'd done something like that, classic acting-out behaviors. I'm kind of a shameful stereotype. No attention from Dad so…anyway, you get the idea. He went away to college. I called about the baby but he…he didn't call back."

"He didn't call you back?"

"We were both young and stupid. He had college to look forward to. A way out of the hellhole we lived in and probably the last thing he wanted was to deal with having a kid back home. It doesn't excuse him but…I'm not mad at him for it. I…did it by myself."

"And after that, that was when you changed your name?"

She nodded, ready to tell now. "I needed to be someone different. I don't know how else to explain it. I just…I couldn't be…that girl anymore. The Johnsons, the adoptive parents, they paid for my prenatal care and my hospital bill, but they also had the agency send me a monetary gift. Something to help me start over. I felt like I had a choice in that moment. To go back to the place I'd always called home. Back to my old friends, who were still wasting any potential they might have had by partying it away. Back to a father who never seemed to notice what was happening with my life. Or I could try and take the fresh start. In that moment, everything seemed… new. For the first time, I felt like I could be anything. Do anything. I changed my name and figured out what I would have to do to get into college. Found the right people to help me forge the transcripts. And then I bought a plane ticket to Barcelona. And then I hit the ground running."

"And you've been running ever since."

She nodded. "I have been." She looked out at the sea, the white-capped waves rolling into the shore. "But I can't run from this."

"Neither can I. It's not in me. This is reality and we have to face it. But I'm certain we can make it work."

"I'm afraid that…it's going to bring it all back. I've spent so many years trying to let go. And it's a process. Like I said, some days I'm thankful. I'm glad for the stable life I'm sure he's had. Glad he's been able to grow up in comfort. Glad I was able to…to make something better of myself. But…"

"Come here." He sat down at the base of one of the trees and leaned against the smooth bark.

Hannah moved to where he was and sat. There was space between them; neither of them looked at each other. "Things are different now, Hannah. We can make this work. We'll do it together."

She put her hand on her stomach. "Can we?"

He put his hand over hers and a spark shot through her. "We will. We'll do it, because you're the strongest woman I've ever met. And I'm…not as much as I used to be but… But in some ways…"

"In some ways better," she said. Thinking of the Eduardo he had been. The laughing, mocking man who had taken nothing seriously.

"Yes, that, too."

She shivered. "I'm afraid of screwing a kid up. Like my parents did to me."

"I don't blame you."

"But your parents love you. You know how it's supposed to be."

He nodded slowly. "Yes. My parents do love me. They, especially my father, were never overly demonstrative, but I always knew that he had my best interests at heart. He made sure we were all cared for. Provided for. He was the pillar of my family. Still, I plagued him. I married an American girl he didn't approve of."

"Not at first," she said, remembering how things had been in the end. How Eduardo's father had told her she had one of the finest minds he'd ever encountered. That she could achieve great things if she kept going. "But in the end…well, before I left you and made him hate me again…he treated me better than almost anyone else in my life. I'll always be grateful to him for his confidence in me."

"You know what you were missing growing up, Hannah, and I truly believe you'll know what needs to be given to your child."

She broke free of him, moving into a standing position.

One thing was certain, she wasn't going to be able to think clearly while he was touching her.

"I hope you're right."

"Every parent starting out is afraid of whether or not they'll be good enough. So I hear."

"What if it affects your work?"

"It won't. I'll make sure that everything is taken care of. If things slip a bit, then they slip."

"But it's not what you want."

"Of course not. It's never been what I wanted. That's why I went to such great lengths to bring you back." A stark reminder that it had been her brains he wanted, not her body. Not that that was a bad thing. Really, it was flattering. Positive even. "I'm completely certain we can put the proper systems in place to ensure that nothing bad happens with the company."

She was glad he was feeling certain about something. She was feeling…dull. Achy. On edge. Far too close to having her past and future collide. To losing the detachment she'd made with that long-ago self.

"I remember his face," she said, not sure why she'd allowed the words to escape.

"Your child?"

She nodded. "He was a boy. They said that when he was born. And they lifted him up and I thought I could turn away quickly enough. That I wouldn't have to see him. That I could pretend it hadn't been real at all. But it was. He was." She blinked hard, trying to keep from dissolving completely. "I'll never forget his face."

"Perhaps you shouldn't."

She shook her head. "I don't want to anymore. But I did for a long time. I wished I could make it go away. Wished I didn't…ache for him. Like something was missing from inside of me."

"Is it like that? Still?"

She swallowed. "In some ways. But…I just…I have to let him go, don't I? I'm not his mother. Not really. I don't even know what they named him. I never held him or kissed him. I didn't watch him take his first steps. Or see him go to school for the first time. I never put a bandage on his scraped knees or…or…" She couldn't breathe. It took her a moment to realize it was because she was sobbing. Great gasps of air that came from deep inside of her and made her feel like she was breaking in two.

She sat down, on her knees in the sand, moisture seeping through the thick denim fabric of her pants. Her throat was burning, raw and painful, like she'd been screaming. But she hadn't been. She'd never allowed herself to let go so much. This was the first time she'd truly cried in years, not just tears, but with every piece of herself. This was the first time she'd cried for her son.

The first time she'd let herself fully realize what she'd lost.

Dimly she was aware of Eduardo hovering near her. He knelt down beside her, not touching her, and she was glad. Because if he did she would melt into him completely.

Finally, the storm passed, almost as quickly as it had hit. She shifted so that she was sitting on her backside, knees drawn up to her chest.

"I never told him I loved him," she said.

"He was a baby, Hannah," Eduardo said, his voice rusty.

"I know but…I don't even think I really let myself feel it." She looked up at him. "I did, though. I do."

"I know," he said.

Eduardo felt like his heart was going to hammer out of his chest. Fear. It was pure fear that had him shaking and on edge. He didn't know what to do with such raw emotion, didn't feel like he had the strength to handle it. What Hannah had been through…it was beyond him. What she had lost…it was so much greater than anything he had lost.

And yet, she knew, and he did, too, that she'd had very little choice.

He moved closer to her, unsure if he should touch her, take her in his arms, or not.

"Hannah, look at all you've accomplished in your life. You made the right choice. For both of you. So you could both live better."

"I know," she said, her voice firm. "I do know. But…just because a choice is right doesn't mean it won't hurt like hell."

"No, that is true."

"It hurts so much to love like this," she said softly. "To love a child. You're never the same again."

Another pang of fear hit him hard. "That's okay."

"You really think so?"

"I have to. No matter what, we've made a baby." She winced. "Sorry, cheesy choice of wording perhaps, but no matter what…there will…most likely be a baby. And we either face giving him up or keeping him. I think…I think we should keep him." The idea terrified him in many ways, but not more than feeling the sort of grief that came from Hannah in palpable waves.

Hannah wrapped her arms around herself like she was cold. "I…I think…"

"We'll do this, Hannah. Together. I'll be with you."

Her pale blue eyes, looking brighter thanks to the red rims they'd acquired during her crying jag, locked with his. "I trust you."

And he knew that that was probably the deepest compliment he had ever received. From Hannah or anyone.

He tried to block out the weight of it. The responsibility he might not be able to live up to. He winced against the pain in his head.

He would do it. He didn't have a choice.

Eduardo lifted his head from the floor. How was it possible for the medicine cabinet to be so far away? After the beach, his headache had steadily gotten worse until every fragment of light, every sound had become excruciating.

And he'd put off going for his medication. Put off acknowledging it because he didn't want Hannah to know.

His vision blurred and another stab of pain went through his head, through his body. Nausea rolled through him and he laid his head back down against the hard tile. He prayed that somehow the cold would work like an ice pack. That it would provide some relief. Enough that he could stand up and get his pills at least.

A fresh wave of pain hit him and he groaned, curling up, trying to shield himself from further attacks. It was impossible. He knew it, but it didn't stop him from trying.

If he could just stand up.

"Eduardo?"

Hannah's voice cut through the door. Cut through his skull. He wanted to tell her to go away, but just imagining the pain that would cause brought the acidic taste of bile to the back of his throat.

"Eduardo?" She was closer now, her voice sharper.

He growled against the floor, planting his hand in front of him, trying to push himself up. He was rewarded with another knife through his skull, so strong it put black spots in his vision.

"Go away, Hannah," he said. A rough sound escaped his lips as another shot of pain cracked through him. It hit him like a wall, the force of it enough to black out his sight entirely. He couldn't see anything. Couldn't move. Couldn't have found his way to the medicine cabinet now even if standing were a possibility.

"Are you okay? You're scaring me."

He pressed his forehead back down on the tile. He took a deep breath, steeling himself for the agony he was about to put himself in. But she couldn't see him. Not like this. On the floor, immobilized, sweating, shaking. Blind.

No. She couldn't see this.

"Go away, Hannah!" he roared, the shock of his own voice lancing him with intense physical torment that started at his head and worked through the rest of him. His face, his cheeks, were wet. From sweat or from unforgivable weakness, he didn't know.

"Eduardo, I am about to open the door. Sorry, but I am. You're freaking me out now."

She pushed the door open and he stretched his hand out, trying to stop it, but he was too weak to lift his arm. He was too weak in every way.

"Oh…are you…are you okay?" Hannah was down beside him, her voice too close, her hand on his face.

He shook his head, trying to find it in him to speak again. She was here. And he needed his pills. "Medicine cabinet," he said.

He heard her stand, the noises she made while rummaging through the medicine cabinet drumming in his head. He heard the water running and Hannah was kneeling beside him again.

Hannah looked down at Eduardo, panic racing through her. He'd mentioned migraines and she hoped that was all this was. Though…there was nothing minor about it, even if the symptoms weren't fatal.

She shifted so that she was sitting on her bottom behind Eduardo's head. Then she gripped him beneath his arms and tugged him up so that his head was resting on her thigh. His face was damp, with sweat and tears and her heart burned for him. His eyes were unfocused, open and staring.

She hated that she was seeing it. Not for her, but for him. Because she knew that this was flaying his pride, killing a part of him that was so essential to him.

She picked up the cup of water she'd set on the floor and tried to angle his head. She opened her hand and he opened his mouth as she put the pills on his tongue. She put the water

glass to his lips and tilted it slowly. He swallowed the pills
and his eyes fluttered closed, his head falling back to her lap.

She set the glass down and leaned back against the tub,
her hands on his chest, feeling the steady beat of his heart
beneath her hands. Every so often his muscles would tense,
his face contorting, and her heart would burn.

The tile started to feel really hard, and the tub wasn't any
better against her back, but she kept sitting there. Kept holding him.

There was nothing, not a sore butt or aching back, that was
going to move her. Because Eduardo was hers. She tightened
her hold on him and took a sharp, halting breath. She didn't
know what that meant, she only knew that he was. That of all
the people in the world, he was the only person who seemed to
understand her. The only person who seemed to want to try.

Eduardo mattered. Her heart started beating faster as the
realization worked its way through her. He mattered more
than work. More than her personal success or her image. *He*
mattered.

The beautiful, broken man in her arms was worth caring
about. And she could. She did. No, he wasn't slick, urbane
Eduardo from five years ago, but she didn't need him to be.
That man hadn't called to her. That man hadn't reached her
heart.

She moved her hand to his forehead and smoothed the lines
there, trying to rub out his concerns. Trying to ease his pain.

Her heart tightened.

Maybe she could do it. Maybe they could do it.

One thing she knew for certain, as she sat there with her
body aching, Eduardo in her arms, was that some people were
worth caring for, worth working for. Eduardo was worth it.
Their baby was worth it.

A sharp sense of longing, of tenderness, hit in her in the
chest. She closed her eyes, letting a tear fall down her cheek.
She lowered her head and rested her forehead on his.

She didn't know anything about marriage. Or about children. Or being a mother. But he made her want to try.

"Hannah?" When Eduardo woke up, it was dark. At least he hoped it was dark. His vision had gone before during migraines, but it never lasted long. He hoped it never did.

The fact that Hannah had seen him at his weakest...it galled him. And yet, he had needed her. That didn't make it feel any better.

"I'm right here," she said. She sounded tired, like she'd been sleeping.

It took him a moment to realize that he was in bed, and that she was sitting a few feet away.

"How did you manage to get me into bed?"

"Ah, gee, Eduardo, I've gotten you into bed a couple of times. I can't say it was all that hard."

"Hannah," he said, moving into a sitting position, every muscle in his body screaming at him, "I'm serious." His eyes started to adjust to the dim room, and he could see her, in his chair, her legs tucked up under her.

"Truthfully? You walked with me...you were just really out of it. And anyway, it's not that far."

"I don't want you to have to deal with things like this...."

"How often does this happen?" she asked.

"Migraines? Once every week or so. Migraines like that? It's been months since I've had to deal with anything on that level. They've gotten further apart but..."

"All this stress."

He shook his head. "Not necessarily."

"I've been thinking."

"You never stop thinking, *querida*."

"Granted. But I've been thinking specifically about our baby. And about our future."

He swallowed. "What about it?"

"We're already married."

"A fact we're both well aware of as it caused you grief a few weeks ago."

She nodded curtly. "Yes, but now I'm thinking it's advantageous."

"How do you mean?"

"We're having a baby."

"So many things manage to slip my mind, Hannah, and yet that one has not."

She laughed, a small, nervous sound. He wasn't used to Hannah sounding nervous. "I know…I— Do you want to talk later? I mean…that was a bad… It was bad. If you don't feel up to talking, I understand."

"Talk, Hannah."

"Okay. I think we should stay married. I think we should be a family."

"A…family? What do you think makes a family, Hannah? Marriage?"

She hopped out of the chair and started pacing. "I don't know, Eduardo. I…I don't really. I've never had a family. But on that note, I can tell you what doesn't make a family. A mother who never comes to see you. A father who can't be bothered to say four words to you on a daily basis. Do you know, he never did one thing for me? He bought frozen dinners and I heated them up for both of us. The school bus made sure I got to school. No one went to my parent-teacher conferences. I…" She took a breath. "I was seven when one of my friends said something about my hair not being brushed before I went to school. She started doing it for me on the bus. So, that's what family isn't. I'd really like to try and make a real family."

His heart hurt, for Hannah. The woman she was now, the little girl she'd been. He wanted to hold her close. Erase every bad thing that had ever happened to her. He wanted to care for her.

And then he remembered the events of the past few hours.

Remembered the fact that Hannah had just spent the afternoon caring for him.

He couldn't give her what she needed, what she deserved.

"Hannah, do you really understand what you just saw? When that happens...I can't move. I can't see. You want to try and make your perfect vision of family with me?"

"You're the one who wanted to try this. And I do, too," she said, conviction infusing her tone. "You said we'd do this together. I want to make this work. And the great thing is, we don't have to do anything. We're already married. We already talked about me coming to live in Barcelona. Really... really, it's perfect."

"And us, Hannah?" His whole body tightened when he thought of the other benefits of Hannah being his wife.

"I..."

Hannah felt like her insides had frozen. Of course sex would come into it. The sex between them was great. No question. And she wanted it, there was no question there, either. And if they were going to be married...well, it was only logical.

Then she thought back to that moment on the floor of the bathroom, when she'd held him in her arms. When she'd felt like he was part of her.

Just the thought of what it would be like to kiss him now, to be skin to skin with him now, when she felt so emotionally raw and stripped bare, when her defenses were gone, frightened her down to her soul.

"I can't think about it right now," she said. "That's just to say...I have to process one thing at a time. You and I will have...all the time ever to figure each other out."

Although, she was afraid she would need that much time just to sort herself out.

"That seems fair," he said, his voice rough.

"So...will you stay married to me?"

"Yes, Hannah," he said.

"Great. Good. That's…great. And good. Do you need anything?"

"No. Just sleep."

"Good, I'll leave you to that, then."

Hannah walked out of Eduardo's room and closed the door behind her. And only then did she realize she'd been holding her breath. She was going to have to get it together. She couldn't risk letting herself fall for him. She'd never believed in love, or at least she'd never believed that she could love anyone. That they could love her.

And she couldn't afford it. Couldn't afford to depend on him like that. To need him so much.

She thought back to that moment of fierce, pure possessiveness she'd felt, kneeling on the bathroom floor with him. That he was hers.

She tried to swallow past the lump in her throat. She would deal with the emotion stuff later. For now, she just had to focus on the positives. She was having a baby; she and Eduardo were doing the best thing possible for their baby. She had a plan.

She inhaled and exhaled slowly. Yes, she had a plan. And when she made plans, she kept them. A plan always fixed things.

Suddenly everything felt much more doable.

CHAPTER TWELVE

HANNAH hit the send button on her email and whimpered inwardly. She'd resigned from her job in San Francisco. Not the first job she'd resigned from. But she'd liked the job. She'd contacted a removal company about clearing out her apartment the day before, and had her now-ex-assistant working on listing the furniture and home for sale.

She was used to leaving, but it still felt strange. Sad.

The door to her new and now-more-permanent office at Vega opened and Eduardo entered on a loud and virulent curse.

"Why are you swearing? I'm the one that just resigned from my job." They'd been back in Barcelona for the whole week and they'd kept things very civilized and organized between them.

There was no mention of resuming a physical relationship. No mention of the future. And no mention of the migraine. She could handle that. Was using the time to try and heal, to try and rebuild her walls. To get a grip on the soft gooeyness that seemed to be overtaking her.

They had their system in place, her in her room, he in his, and they came to work together. And, it had even been decided she would be the new financial manager at Vega.

So, all in all, a good week. Even if she did feel confused and lonely. And a little nauseous.

"There's a…charity dinner tonight and I forgot about it. I

had it in my calendar but then I forgot to sync the calendar and so it didn't end up on my phone."

"Tonight?"

"Yes, after work."

"Well, that's not so bad. Go put on a tux and mingle for a couple of hours. It won't kill you."

"I'm not fun."

"You're not…boring."

"You have to come with me."

"No thanks."

"Hannah Vega, you have to come with me, because you are my wife. And my company and the success of it, is very important to you. Which means, the appearance of stability in my life should be very important to you. This is your son's or daughter's legacy, after all."

"Don't be a bear, Eduardo."

"I don't know another way to be. I told you, I'm not fun."

Her cheeks heated as she thought of some of the ways she'd had fun with Eduardo. Oh, no, she was not going there. No, no, no. "You'll be fine. We'll be fine. Not sure I'm up to going out, looking saucy and conspicuously avoiding drinking the champagne, but hey, why not?"

His expression lightened suddenly, concern filling his dark eyes. "I'm sorry, I didn't consider you might not be feeling up to it. I…forgot."

"Don't worry about it. I'm more worried about you. You're up to it?"

His expression darkened. "I'm fine."

"Good. Just tell me what color to wear, and I'll be ready by…when do you need?"

"Eight."

"Eight. I'm good at these kinds of things."

"I know you are," he said, his eyebrows drawing together a bit.

She wanted to go and touch him, comfort him. She wasn't

all that great at comforting people, not historically anyway, but she wanted to. Although, she wasn't sure what was allowed in the neutral zone that was their relationship. They weren't any closer than they'd been a week ago. They hadn't fought more, either. She actually missed fighting with him. Missed the spike of passion that had been between them in some form from the moment they'd met.

She missed the sex even more.

"So, just reap the benefits then and stop looking like the world is crumbling all around you." She stood up and took her purse off the hook behind her desk. "So, what color do you need me to wear?"

"Why?"

"I need to go shopping."

Something in his expression changed, darkened. Went back to how it had been before. And she liked it. "Wear red," he said.

She looked him up and down, heat firing in her blood. "Yeah. Maybe."

She swept past him and walked out of the office.

Eduardo was in hell. He was with the hottest woman in the room, in any room on the planet, he was certain, and yet, she was off-limits to him. Because she needed time to think about where things would go between them. Hell, he needed time. They weren't in a position to have a fun, heated affair. They were married. They were going to be parents.

It wasn't that he couldn't touch her. He had to touch her. She was his wife, and they were playing the reconciliation game. He realized that in many ways they were now playing it for life. No one was to suspect they weren't the loving couple they appeared to be. That he slept alone, with a hard-on that wouldn't quit.

Everyone had to see a committed, devoted couple. The press, most especially, had to see a committed, devoted couple.

But with Hannah dressed in a slinky red dress, with only one strap that gathered at her shoulder like a bow and made her look like a particularly tempting present, her curves hugged close and displayed perfectly by the close fit of the gown, the game was torture. And a simple touch wasn't enough.

"That dress makes quite the statement," he said, his eyes on the elegant curve of her neck. She was scanning the room, looking for the most influential people. At least, he imagined that's what she was doing. She had that way about her. Like she was always on alert. Always on show.

"That was the idea. And it matches your tie." She turned to face him, feathering her fingertips over the silk fabric of his necktie.

"I doubt anyone has noticed my tie."

"It's impossible not to notice a hot man in a great suit," she said, blue eyes raking over him, the appreciation in them open and undisguised. "So trust me, you've been noticed."

"To what do I owe the compliment?"

"Just honesty." Her smile widened and she took a step forward, bringing him with her as she intercepted an older man with a date some twenty years his junior.

They made casual conversation with him, Hannah enquiring after the man's grown children, asking him about his business. Eduardo followed her lead and managed to engage both the man and his date, whom he introduced as Laura, in a steady conversation for a few moments before they both moved on.

When they left, he frowned and leaned in to Hannah. "Why didn't he introduce himself?"

Hannah looked at him, her eyes wide. "That was Carlo Caretti."

He knew the name, and worse, he had the sinking feeling he'd met the man. On more than one occasion. In fact, several occasions. "He's placed some very large orders with

Vega for exclusive mobile phones for Caretti International," he said, everything slotting into place.

"Yes. He's a very big client for you. Has been for years."

"I haven't seen him since…"

"I know. It's fine. You covered fine."

He set his glass of champagne down. Hannah wasn't drinking; she couldn't drink. So he shouldn't, either. Which reminded him that he'd forgotten to ask how she felt.

"How are you?"

She waved her hand. "I'm fine."

"Not tired?"

"No. I like parties. Well, parties like this." She laughed. "Sort of over the whole high school undercover kegger."

"Been to a few, have you?"

She tossed him a look. "My former self? Yes. She enjoyed them. They made her forget how sad she was. Hannah Weston? No, she doesn't like them much."

Her admission hit him hard. More aching sadness for the strong, beautiful woman he called his wife. "What about Hannah Vega?"

"I haven't changed my name."

He frowned. "Will you?"

She blinked rapidly. "I…I hadn't really thought about it."

Another couple stopped and chatted with them for a while and thankfully, he'd never met them so he didn't feel stupid when they left. "I really didn't know them, right?" he asked, checking with Hannah.

She shook her head. "I don't think so. If you did, I don't know why, so they can't be that important. Ack, that sounds mean."

"Well, that's how you see things isn't it? In terms of business value."

She frowned. "Generally. I'm not sure I like it."

"I don't mind it."

"I don't see everything that way," she said, and he knew she meant the baby.

"I know you don't."

She bit her lip and nodded slowly. He wrapped his arm tightly around her waist and led her deeper into the opulent ballroom. People were milling around, looking at the artwork on the wall, placing written bids that were much higher than any of the work was worth. But proceeds went to a children's hospital charity and that meant generosity was high, and very few people actually cared what it was they were bidding on.

Hannah stopped in front of a painting of a woman. The woman was on a busy street, in a crowd. She was facing a different direction to everyone else, and there was space around her, while all the other people in the picture nearly blurred together into an indistinguishable mass.

"She's special," he said. She certainly stood out. She reminded him of Hannah. A woman who could never simply blend.

"She looks lonely to me," Hannah said.

He turned to look at her. She was staring at the painting, her attention rapt. "No one is touching her. No one's going with her."

"But she stands out," he said.

"By herself."

He extended his hand and brushed his thumb across her cheek. She turned to face him, eyes wide. "She's not alone."

She blinked. "I...I want to bid on this one." She took a slip of paper from the podium and wrote down a number she hid from him, then dropped the folded white square into the box.

"I think I'll place a bid, too." He got his own slip of paper and wrote his own bid on it. He was certain he would beat her. And then he would give it to her.

"You look confident there, Eduardo."

"I am," he said, dropping his bid into the box. "I think I'll win."

"Do you?"

"I do."

"A wager then."

"A wager?"

"Mmm-hmm. If I win, I get a favor. If you win, you get a favor."

"A favor?"

"A foot rub, a half day at work. Something. Be imaginative."

"I don't know if I'm imaginative."

"I'm sure you can be," she said.

"All right then, I take your bet."

She extended her hand and he shook it, then he leaned down and pressed his lips to her knuckles. Heat shot through him, down to his gut, gripping him tight with fiery fingers.

"Good," she said, her tone light, breathless. "When do they announce the winners?"

He checked his watch and the sign on the podium. "Bidding is closed in five minutes and it looks like they'll take about thirty minutes to announce the winners."

"Then we have some mingling time."

He could have groaned at that, but he kept his mind busy thinking of just what he would ask of her when he got his favor. A kiss maybe. More. The image of her lips on his body, on his shaft, as she'd done the first night they were together haunted him, intoxicated him.

They'd been strictly hands-off for the past week, and for good reason. And it was likely she hadn't intended the favor to be sexual, but damned if he could think of anything else.

He would ask for something else when he won. But for now he would let his mind wander.

The announcement was five minutes late, and in that space of five minutes he was more aware of the time than he'd been in his recent memory.

The man who was orchestrating the evening started reading off the auction winners and directing them to go to the back of the room to write their checks.

"Lot number fourteen goes to Hannah Vega," he said, barely taking a breath before moving on to fifteen.

Hannah shot him a triumphant smile. "I win." She breezed away from him, going to write her check and claim her spoils, he imagined. He followed after her.

"What did you bid?"

"A lot," she said, smiling sweetly.

"Why?"

"I can. I have a lot of money, Eduardo. But you know that."

"I know it, but I didn't know you were the type."

"I very much am. I give a lot to charity. And I really liked the painting."

"It looked like it made you sad."

She shrugged. "I connected with it. I'm going to hang it in our house."

"How much was your bid?" he repeated.

She gave him a figure that made his brows raise. They reached the back table and she dashed off a check and handed it to the woman manning the station.

"Would you like it delivered, Señora Vega?"

Hannah nodded. "I would, thank you." She bent and scribbled his address on a piece of paper. "To this address, please."

Eduardo took his own checkbook out and wrote a check for double what Hannah had bid on the painting. "I would like to add a contribution," he said, setting it on the table.

She lifted a brow but didn't say anything until they walked away. "Big man," she said.

"It's for a good cause, Hannah."

"Yes, but you mainly did it to show me up."

He shrugged. "I don't want people thinking you had to be the one to bid and pay."

"Does it matter?"

"Of course it does. I'm your husband, I'm supposed to take care of you."

She raised a brow and pursed her lips. "Oh, really. Well, all right then. I'm just glad you donated."

"Are you ready to go?"

She nodded. "If you are."

"I was ready to leave before we got here."

She laughed and took hold of his arm, giving little finger waves to everyone they passed by. "Don't look like such a storm cloud."

He forced a smile. "Better?" he asked.

"Much better," she said through her teeth.

They took a car back to his penthouse and she didn't make a mention of her favor the whole ride there. She was uncharacteristically quiet. Hannah was not known for her quiet.

When they got inside she leaned against the door, staring off into space, chewing her bottom lip.

"You must be tired," he said.

"A bit."

"Me, too. I'm going to head to bed. I'll see you in the morning, Hannah." After tonight, with her in that dress, with all of the touching and teasing that had happened at the charity event, it took every ounce of his strength to keep from going and kissing her.

"Wait," she said, just as he turned his back.

"What is it?" He turned to her, his heart pounding heavily.

"You still owe me a favor."

CHAPTER THIRTEEN

HANNAH felt like she was going to shake apart. At least, the shaking seemed to be happening from the inside out. There was small consolation in the fact that when she pushed off from the door and took a step toward him, her limbs didn't tremble.

"You're not getting out of it so easily," she said.

"Granting you your favor?"

She nodded, still not quite sure how she was going to execute the next part of her plan. Not quite sure when it had become her plan. She was hazy on the whole thing. But sometime between putting the huge figure down on her auction sheet and getting in the car with Eduardo, his heat so close to her she felt like she was burning up, she'd decided that her favor was going to involve getting him back into her arms. Back into her bed.

To what end? Oh, that she wasn't sure about.

About the only thing she was sure about was how much she wanted him. And she was ready to act on it.

"First things first, how much did you have to drink tonight?" she asked.

He lifted his chin, one dark brow lifted. "Why?"

"I'm stone-cold sober, a side effect of pregnancy, and I refuse to take advantage of a drunk man."

"I'm as sober as you are."

She nodded. "Excellent." She sounded so calm. Her voice

was odd to her own ears because it simply didn't match the jittery, fearful excitement that was rolling through her body. She looked around the penthouse, trying to plan her next move, trying to figure out what to ask him to do.

She closed her eyes and shook her head. She wasn't planning it. She was just going with what she wanted.

The idea of Eduardo as her personal playground was fairly enticing. The idea of getting just what she wanted from him. No-holds-barred access. She was on board with that.

She walked toward him, her heart pounding hard. "Take off your tie."

He raised his hand to the red knot at the base of his throat and paused. "Is that the favor? Because I was going to do this up in my room anyway."

"No. My favor comes in stages."

"Is that allowed?"

She smiled, a flush of warmth suffusing her. "Maybe not. But I'm up for a little rule breaking. How about you?"

He didn't move and for a moment, she was afraid he would say that he wasn't in the mood to break any rules. That they needed to keep things bland and passive and safe between them.

Then he started working the knot on the tie, the bit of red silk sliding down the front of his black jacket and pooling on the floor. He stood, waiting. For another command.

"Jacket," she said.

He obeyed.

"Now your shirt."

She watched, her heart in her throat as he undid the buttons at his cuffs, then worked the buttons at the front of the shirt, consigning it to the floor, as well. She was happy for the chance to look at him with the light on, to really take in the sight of his body. The sculpted, well-defined muscles, his broad masculine frame.

Just looking at him made her breasts ache, her nipples

tighten. She'd never wanted like this. Never before him, never in the years during their separation. She knew she never would again.

He put his hands on his belt and her eyes fell to the very clear outline of his erection. She sucked in a sharp breath. "Not yet."

He removed his hands. His eyes glittering in challenge. He was enjoying the game, she could tell. But she was also willing to bet he was waiting for the right moment to reverse it.

The thought sparked a flicker of heat low in her belly.

"Go sit on the couch."

He turned and walked toward the couch and she followed, her eyes on his backside.

"Checking me out?" he asked, sitting on the smooth leather couch, draping his arms across the back of it.

"Absolutely. And now I'm trying to decide what to do with you next."

She put her hands behind her back and gripped the tab of her zipper, lowering it slightly. The strap of her dress slipped, dropped so that the top fell dangerously low, draped over her breast, coming close to revealing the gossamer red bra she had beneath it.

Eduardo's face tensed, his hands curling into fists. He didn't move.

She arched and tugged the zipper down farther, letting the dress fall to her waist.

She heard his breath release in a sharp hiss.

"More?" she asked.

"You're the boss," he said, teeth gritted.

She smiled and brought the zipper down the rest of the way, letting the dress slide down her hips and pool at her feet. Showing him her thigh-high stockings and matching lace bra and panty set.

She walked over to the couch and sat next to him, his heat

warming her, the hunger in his gaze erasing any unease she might feel.

She put her hands on his chest and ran her fingertips over his finely sculpted muscles. And she didn't want to play games anymore.

"You're the sexiest man I've ever seen," she said, dipping her head and running her tongue over his nipple. He reached up and forked his fingers through her hair, holding her to him.

She pressed a kiss to his stomach, tight and flat, utter perfection. "I'm the luckiest woman alive, no question."

He laughed hoarsely. "I don't know about that, but I must be the luckiest man."

She put her hands on his belt buckle. "I've been told my mouth gets me into trouble."

"I would love to see that for myself," he said, voice tight.

She smiled and worked at his belt, then the closure of his pants. He helped her pull them off and then he was naked in front of her. She gripped his erection, squeezing, watching his head fall back, reveling in how labored his breathing became.

She leaned in and tasted him, gratified by the harsh sound of pleasure that escaped his lips. She pleasured him that way until he was shaking, until a fine sheen of sweat covered his olive skin.

"Hannah," he said roughly, "not yet, Hannah. Please."

She lifted her head and pressed a kiss to his stomach. "Not yet?"

"Not like that. I thought I owed you the favor?"

She laughed. "I didn't do anything I didn't want." She straightened and leaned in, kissing him on the lips, deep, passionate, pouring everything into it.

When they broke apart, they were both breathing hard. He held her chin between his thumb and forefinger, his dark eyes burning into hers. She felt a response in her chest, a strange tightness that made it hard to breathe. She wanted to cry, and laugh at the same time.

Instead, she kissed him again and he pulled her into his lap, his hands roaming over her curves, mouth and fingers teasing, tormenting, bringing her to the edge and then easing her back, building and retreating, the most perfect torture she could imagine.

She planted her hands on his shoulders, pressing herself tight up against him, his erection teasing her right where she was wet and ready for him.

He pressed a kiss to her collarbone, trailed a line with his tongue down to where the flimsy lace bra met the rounded curve of her breasts.

At the same time, he pushed his finger beneath the lacy edge of her panties and slid the tip of it over her clitoris, the strokes sending white heat through her, ramping up her arousal. She whimpered, tucked her head against his neck, kissing him there.

"I can't wait anymore," she said, her voice shaking. Gone was the control, the steadiness. She didn't have any of it now. She was too filled with her need for him to think, or seem cool. To wait to get the rest of her clothes off, her shoes off.

He tugged her panties to the side and pushed up inside of her. She gasped and arched against him as he filled her. The race to the peak was furious and fast. Eduardo gripped her hips pulling her down onto him as he thrust into her, his movements hard, lacking in finesse, utterly perfect.

She didn't want his control, because she didn't have any. She didn't want evidence of practiced sexual technique. She didn't want anything but him, out of control and just as dizzy with need for her as she was for him. She moved against him, tension drawing tight as a bowstring inside of her until it snapped, releasing her, letting her fall over the edge into bliss, her pleasure washing over her, leaving her spent, consumed in the aftermath.

He thrust up into her one last time, his fingers biting into her flesh, her name a harsh groan on his lips as he found his release.

He rested his head against hers, his breath harsh and hot, fanning over her cheek. Her arms wrapped around his neck, he lifted his hand, pushing her hair, which had come completely unpinned, from her face. His hands were shaking.

She leaned in and rested her head on his shoulder and he held her. While she held him. She never wanted to move. She just wanted to rest with him. She realized that the lights were on, bright and revealing. That she'd just lost her composure in his arms, utterly and completely, and that she wasn't embarrassed at all.

She'd been so afraid of a moment like this. Of being without her trappings. Without her makeup, and sleek hair. Without that suit of armor she kept on at all times. Keeping herself under tight control so that she would never, ever become that wild, stupid girl she'd been when she was growing up.

But she suddenly realized that she wasn't that girl anymore. She'd changed. She wasn't just stomping her down, or covering her up. But she had been holding down the real Hannah Weston. Choking the life out of her because she was so afraid.

So afraid of what? Of being hurt. Of caring.

Of loving.

And now, here she was, with the one man who knew her secrets, caring. Caring so much she felt as if it was pouring from her like blood. But she didn't feel as if it was running out, didn't feel as if it was leaving her weak.

She felt stronger than she had in a long time. Maybe stronger than she ever had. And she wasn't dressed for a business meeting; she wasn't giving someone the steely eye. She was mostly naked, curled up against Eduardo, on the edge of tears.

"Do you need me to move?" she asked, inhaling deeply, the scent of him filling her, making her chest feel like it was expanding.

"No," he said, tightening his hold on her.

"Mmm…good." She kissed his neck again. "I suppose things have the potential to get complicated now. But, on the plus side, the sex between us is very good."

He laughed, shaking beneath her, the low rumble sending a little thrill of pleasure through her. "You could say that."

"That will work, though. This will work."

"Hannah, you think too much. And at the moment, I can't think at all."

"Okay, I'll stop thinking." She shifted to the side and he put his hand on her stomach. She looked down at where his palm was, spread over her pale skin.

They looked up, eyes clashing, her heart squeezed.

"When I look at your face I keep expecting to see the girl I first met five years ago," he said. "In fact, I was counting on it."

"What do you mean?"

"I thought that by bringing you back…I thought if I had you back in my house, in my office, in my life, I might remember what made me blackmail you into marrying me in the first place. The height of my entitlement. An act that so epitomized who I used to be. I thought if I could understand it, feel it again…"

"You were trying to go back," she said.

"Yes. But it didn't work, Hannah. Because I don't see you the same way now. Everything then…everything I was… it was about how it could benefit me. How people could be used to make my life more comfortable. More entertaining. I looked at you and saw a chance to play a game. Now I look and I see you. The real you."

Hannah blinked, trying to stop her eyes from stinging. "I think you're the only one who ever has."

He lifted his hand and looked down at her stomach, a faint frown visible on his face. He traced one faded, white line with the tip of his finger.

"Stretch marks," she said, for once not feeling cagey or weird about the past. "I got them pretty bad with…with him."

"Signs of your strength," he said, his voice rough.

"Or my weakness."

"Never that, Hannah. You are the strongest woman I've ever known. Everyone makes mistakes, but it takes someone truly great to go on and succeed in spite of them."

"I always think I succeeded because of them," she said, voicing a thought she'd never spoken out loud before. "Because getting pregnant the first time forced me to look at myself. To realize I was no better than my parents, who I despised so much. That I was just as irresponsible. That I would repeat the cycle unless I did something to break out of it."

"You did."

She nodded slowly. "Yes." More than that though, she felt like she'd only just really broken out. Yes, she'd gone and gotten an education. And yes, she'd gone and made money. But until this very moment, she doubted that she'd ever really cared for anyone. She doubted she'd ever loved.

She looked up at Eduardo again. She did now. She loved him.

"I…" She found she couldn't speak.

"I think it's time we took this to bed," he said. "And you can lose the shoes." He reached down and disposed of her spiky black heels. "The rest I'll be happy to take care of for you."

He lifted her up and she held on to him tight, unable to take her eyes off him, unable to stop turning over the immense, tender feeling that was spreading from her chest through the rest of her body.

She loved Eduardo. Love was different than she'd imagined.

It was better.

Two weeks passed and every night, Eduardo had Hannah in his bed. Every day, he tried to go to work and concentrate on what he was supposed to do. Sometimes he was more successful than others. He wasn't sure how much of it to blame on his new, unimproved brain and how much to blame on Hannah herself.

She was soft as silk, pale and perfect. The image of her, the thought of how her skin felt beneath his fingertips, seemed to invade his mind constantly. The taste of her, the overwhelming sensation of right when he slid inside of her wet heat.

Even now, as they waited at the exclusive doctor's office, his thoughts were on what was beneath the yellow silk dress she was wearing. Well, his thoughts were bouncing back and forth between that, and the health of their baby.

She was getting things confirmed today and it was enough to have him on edge. The pregnancy had been unintentional, but as they walked into the plush office he felt everything in him seize up and the realization of how important the baby had become to him hit him fully.

The nurse left them in the room and Hannah slipped out of her clothes, tugging a white linen hospital gown on over her body before lying back on the bed.

"Feeling good?" he asked, moving to stand by her head.

"Yeah," she said, her eyes wide. She looked nervous. The sight made his heart wrench up tight. He wasn't used to Hannah being nervous. Lately she'd been…softer. Not in an emotional wreck kind of way, but in a way that made her seem more real. More human. A way that made him want to protect her, shield her from the world. A way that made him want to hold her close and never let her go.

The doctor came in a few moments later and explained the Doppler machine to him before lifting Hannah's hospital gown and squirting a bit of clear gel onto her flat stomach.

"I see this isn't your first pregnancy, Hannah," Dr. Cordoba said.

Hannah shook her head. "No."

"Everything healthy with the last one?"

"Yes," Hannah said, her voice strong. Eduardo wanted to hug her. Kiss her. Tell her how brave she was.

"Good. Very good to know." The woman put the Doppler on Hannah's stomach, moved it lower. It made a kind of strange, white noise sound, changing slightly as she adjusted position.

His eyes were glued to Hannah's, even more specifically, to the little crease between her eyebrows. And then the sound changed to a fast, whooshing sound and the look on her face changed, a smile spreading her lips.

"That's it," she said, reaching for his hand.

He just stood and listened to the sound of his baby's heart filling the room. Listened to it all become real. To every intention of nannies and detachment vanishing, evaporating like smoke.

He felt like he was in a cloud, lost to reality, for the rest of the appointment. Everything was on track. She should come back next month. They'd do a sonogram to get measurements and confirm dates.

They walked out of the doctor's office and back out to the car, and he was thankful that today he'd used a driver. His head was too full to even consider driving at the moment.

He opened Hannah's door for her and settled in beside her. She leaned over and wrapped her arms around him, a sweet smile on her lips. "He's okay," she said. "I'm so glad I…I think part of me was afraid that…"

He wrapped his arm around her, even as fear flooded his chest. "You don't have to be afraid, Hannah."

"I know. Can we…can we stop by a courier's office?"

"Of course, what do you need?"

"I need…" She pulled her purse onto her lap and took a white envelope out, handing it to him. "I want to send this. I… Would you read it?"

He opened up the envelope and took out a handwritten letter. He swallowed hard when he started reading, a lump settling in his throat that stayed with him through the entire letter.

It was to her son. A letter telling him about her circumstances. Telling him that she thought of him. That she hoped he was well. That she loved him.

"It's going to the adoption agency," she said. "That way if he ever wonders about me, he can go look at it but…but if he doesn't…then…I don't want to interrupt his life."

"I think it's perfect, Hannah," he said, his chest feeling tight.

"It's everything I felt like I needed to say. Everything I thought he might want to know. Mostly, I needed him to know that he wasn't unwanted. And that…that he has an extra person in the world who loves him and thinks about him."

He kissed her head. "Two."

"Two?"

"I'll think of him now. Always."

She smiled. "Thank you."

He nodded and brought her close to his body, ignoring the rush of fear that was burning through him. Reading Hannah's letter to a child she barely knew, seeing how much she loved him, even now, made him understand something that he hadn't wanted to understand.

A child would change things. It would change him.

And then there was Hannah. And somewhere, in all of that, was Vega. He was the man who was supposed to take care of all of that.

He closed his eyes and gritted his teeth, fighting hard against the migraine that was threatening to take him over again.

CHAPTER FOURTEEN

"EDUARDO, do you have the quarterly reports in from the retail stores?"

Hannah walked into his office looking every inch the cool businesswoman she was. Different, too. Her face glowed with...happiness.

She was a force of it. He couldn't ignore her, and he didn't want to.

He looked back at his computer screen and closed the window on the internet browser. He'd been looking at colleges. For their son or daughter who was a tiny embryo at that very moment.

He blinked and redirected his focus. "What?"

"The quarterly reports. I need them. Finances. Dollar signs. The thing you pay me for. I just need you to forward them to me. Last week. But unless you have a blue police box capable of time travel, I'll let it go."

"What?"

"Never mind. Do you have the reports or not?"

"I...somewhere. Hold on. They have to be in my in-box somewhere." She was watching him, her blue eyes trained on him. He waited to see impatience, and there was none. She was simply waiting. "Sorry, I'm not right on top of it, Hannah, I know you would be."

She waved a hand. "It's fine. I already did everything else

I had to do today. Anyway, I missed you, so it's nice to come and visit for a while."

She walked over to the desk, her delicate fingers resting on the wood, tracing idly over the designs in the grain. He gritted his teeth and tried to refocus his attention. He swore and slammed his hand down by his keyboard. Hannah jumped.

"I can't find them."

"Do a search."

Of course. He knew that. His mind was moving too slowly, and Hannah was too large in it. He couldn't focus. "Dammit, Hannah, do you mind not hovering?"

She frowned and he could have stabbed his own hand with a pen. "I'm sorry," he said, his voice rough.

"Are you having a hard time? Just let me find it for you."

"It's an email search. I can handle it." He typed in quarterly reports and it brought them up. Suddenly it was like the fog had cleared. He forwarded them to Hannah. "There, you have them now."

"Thank you."

"I'll see you when I'm through here."

She nodded, her lips turned down now. "Okay. See you."

She turned and walked out of his office and he leaned back in his chair, drawing his hand down his face. He was sweating. Why had that been so hard? Why had he forgotten the reports in the first place?

It was the distractions. All the time. All he could think about were Hannah and the baby. And when he wasn't thinking about them, he seemed to want to be thinking about them. So he found excuses to go to Hannah's office, he used Google to look up colleges and real estate listings in the city limits that weren't sky-high penthouses.

He'd thought he could do this. He had to do it. If he didn't, what legacy was there for his son or daughter? It mattered now, even more that he hang on to Vega. It wasn't about personal pride, it was about inheritance. About his child's right to not have their fool of a father destroy what could have been theirs.

Yes, he had a private fortune, but it was much less valuable than what he had here. The potential with Vega Communications was untapped. He knew it could be more. He'd always intended to make it more when his father was running it, and he knew it now. But if he continued to do stupid things like forgetting to forward financial reports, none of it would happen.

Hannah would have to remind him. Hold his hand. She was his wife, and he was meant to care for her. But he wasn't doing his job. He was failing her. He would fail her, continually. Until death did them part. He had tied her to him, to a deficient man, when she was exceptional, brave and bright, brilliant beyond any he'd ever known.

He was sure that when he'd intercepted her on her wedding day she'd wished him to hell a thousand times. But for the first time, he wished himself there.

Eduardo was still tense when they got back to the penthouse. Tense didn't even begin to cover it. She was almost afraid to say anything for fear he would explode. Not that she couldn't handle him. But she was getting the increasingly worrying feeling that he wasn't happy. And that bothered her.

Because she was happy. Going to bed with him every night, waking up with him every morning. It was more than she'd ever imagined marriage to be. What he made her feel when he touched her was divine, but more than that was the connection between them.

She'd been skin to skin with men, boys really, before. She'd had lovers, if they could be called that. But she'd picked up and left them when they were through and felt…nothing. It had frightened her sometimes. When she was with them, she'd gotten the thrill, but it hadn't lingered, and they had never lingered in her mind, and certainly never her heart.

But Eduardo…he felt like he was a part of her. And she knew, knew for a fact, it had nothing to do with carrying his baby. She'd felt no mystical pull to the boy who'd gotten her pregnant the first time. No sense that she had a piece of him with her.

No, Eduardo was utterly unique and so was the connection she felt to him. It was deeper than sex. In fact, it had existed before the sex.

When the door closed behind them, he didn't speak, he just pulled her into his arms. His kiss was rough and demanding, his hands roaming over her curves, tugging at her shirt, her skirt. She pushed his jacket down his arms and onto the floor, devouring his mouth, conducting an exploration of her own.

They left a trail of clothes on their way to his bedroom. His movements were urgent, his mouth hard and hungry.

"There are ways I can care for you that no other man can," he said, his voice rough as he laid her down onto the bed. "There are things I can do." He put his hand down between her thighs and slid his fingers over the damp folds of her flesh. "Things I can make you feel, that no other man can make you feel."

She could only nod as he slid one finger inside of her.

"You want me?" he asked.

She nodded, her breath coming out on a sob. "Of course."

"Say it."

She opened her eyes, met with his intense, dark gaze. "I want you, Eduardo Vega. My husband."

A smile curved his mouth and he lowered his head, sucking hard on her nipple before continuing down, his mouth hot and demanding on her body, making her feel restless, so turned on she couldn't think or breathe.

When his mouth covered the heart of her she couldn't do anything but ride the wave of pleasure that threatened to carry her away.

Eduardo was drowning in her scent, her taste. His body

was on fire, his heart threatening to beat from his chest. He felt her tense beneath him, felt her body tighten as she found her release.

He pressed a kiss to her stomach and put his hand under her bottom, lifting her so that he could enter her in one smooth thrust. She arched against him, a hoarse cry escaping her lips that he captured with his own.

She was so tight and hot around him, her legs pinning him against her body, her small breasts, tight nipples, pressing into his chest. She tightened around his shaft and he just about lost it then and there. But he was going to make her come one more time.

He thrust hard into her and she tightened her hold on him, pressed wet kisses to his neck, whispering in his ear. How sexy he was. How good he felt.

And his blood roared in his ears, all thoughts of control and finesse lost in the rising tide of pleasure and urgency that was flooding him.

His orgasm overtook him like wildfire, impossible to stop, impossible to redirect, consuming everything in its path. He let out a short, sharp sound of pleasure as he spilled himself inside of her and he was aware, dimly, of Hannah shuddering out her own release.

He rested his head on her breasts, waited for his heart rate to return to normal. Waited for thoughts to start trickling through his brain.

All he had now was an intense emotion that seemed to be filling his chest. That seemed to be taking over.

He turned his face, inhaled her scent, let it fill him. She stroked his face, her hands soft, her touch soothing him down deep.

And he realized that no matter how many orgasms he'd given her, no matter how many he gave her over a lifetime, it wasn't proof that he was caring for her. Even now he was starving for her, for what she could give him. To have her arms around him, to have her hold him close.

And when the time came for another migraine, when he was curled up on the floor, unable to see, barely able to breathe, she would be the one who would have to hold him.

He would be a dead weight to her. To all she'd worked for. One more thing to hold Hannah back in life.

He would be damned if he did that to her. Of course, it was entirely possible he already was.

"You look extra broody this morning," Hannah said, walking into the kitchen and seeing Eduardo sitting at the table, his expression dark.

He lifted his cup of coffee to his lips and offered her a bored look.

"That's all you've got for me? At least say something rude," she said, rifling through the fridge for a bottle of milk. She liked that it was only the two of them living in the penthouse. He had staff that came in while they were gone, but otherwise it was just the two of them.

"Hannah, we need to talk."

She straightened then shut the fridge, the milk bottle clutched tightly in her hand. "What about?"

"About this arrangement."

"What about it?" She turned and opened one of the cabinets, reaching for a bowl, ignoring the unease that was making her stomach tighten.

"It's not working."

She dropped the cereal bowl she'd just grasped onto the counter and it clattered loudly against the hard surface, thankfully not shattering. "What?" She grabbed the bowl and stopped it from shivering against the tile. "I mean wh-what about it isn't working? The amazing, soul-shaking sex? The relative harmony in which we live?"

"It's not that. It's... You were right. I'm not doing a good job of balancing domestic life with Vega and it has to change. It's going to get even harder when the baby's born."

"But…Eduardo…"

"I think it would be best if we kept things as simple as possible. Perhaps…perhaps it would be best if we didn't try to force a marriage between us. I've been looking for houses outside the city, but still close. A place more suitable to raising children. I would be happy to install you there with the child and a nanny. I could stay here during the work week."

"What? That doesn't make any sense, it doesn't… I mean… How can we…be a family if you don't even live with us?"

He stood up, slammed his palm down on the table, his expression thunderous. "I am not the man you should cast in your little sitcom, Hannah. I cannot give you whatever your vision is of what a perfect family should look like."

She gripped the edge of the counter, her heart pounding as she listened to him. Was that what she was doing? Was she trying to project her idea of perfection onto him? To force an idea that possibly wasn't real? Had that been what all of it was? Her trying to build a new fantasy?

The sharp pain in her heart told her no. That her feelings were real.

"You think you know the way the world works, Hannah," he continued, his voice a low growl. "You named yourself after a retail store because you thought it was fancy. You think black-and-white television shows are an example of how real life should work. That we can put a picket fence around the yard and get a dog and you can have all the things you've always fantasized about. You play so sophisticated, but in so many ways you're naive. A little girl playing dress-up."

"Is that what you think?" she said, her voice soft, anger rising up inside of her. Unreasonable, and unstoppable. And with it, pain, pain that she felt down so deep she wasn't sure she would ever find the bottom of it. "I'm going to let you have it now, Eduardo Vega, but this isn't just me spouting pithy one-liners to keep you from getting close. This is me being honest. I gave myself to you, and that wasn't pretend. That wasn't something I didn't understand, and you damn well gave yourself to me. So, now what? You're scared? You're freaked out because you forgot to hit Send on an email and now you're letting it get in your head."

"That's not all," he said, his voice fierce. "You know how bad it gets. You've seen."

"Yes, you had a migraine. A horrible one. You have them… I get it. But if I can handle it, then it's not up to you to say that I can't. You're making up excuses, and blaming things, blaming me, blaming you, for the fact that you're just scared because whatever this is between us…it's big. And you're scared of it."

"I'm going to get ready for work now, Hannah. You can call my driver and he'll take you later."

"Are you running?" she asked.

He whirled around to face her, his expression dark, dangerous. "I'm not running. I'm being reasonable. What did you think this would be?" he asked, his voice raw. "You're right. I can barely concentrate on the duties I already have. I don't have it in me, not the energy or the desire to be a husband to you. I can't…I can't take care of you."

Pain washed through Hannah, acute and sharp. "You don't…want to be my husband?"

"No, Hannah," he said, something in his tone jagged. Torn.

"Okay."

"What?"

She shook her head. "Fine. Okay. Then I don't want you to be my husband. I'm not going to force it. It's funny…I was ready to marry Zack even though…even though he didn't know me. He didn't even especially want me. I mean…we weren't really lighting things on fire with our passion, you know? But that was okay with him. It's not okay with you and I only just realized that."

"What do you mean?"

"I won't be a duty to you. I want you to divorce me. And you be the best father you can be for our child. But I'm not going to be that wife you have to keep because you feel some sense of duty."

"All or nothing then."

"Yes." It broke her to say it, because there was a piece of her, that girl who was searching for permanent, for stable, who wanted desperately to cling to whatever he could give. Who wanted to marry the facade and forget the rest.

But the new Hannah, the one Eduardo had brought out, uncovered after so many years, she wanted more. She wanted it all. Not just duty, but love. Real love, not just a few hours of mindless pleasure every night. She wanted to share more than his bed. She wanted to share his heart. His life.

"Then it has to be nothing."

He turned and walked out of the room and she stood, watching the spot where he'd been, adjusting to him not being there.

When he got home from work, Hannah was gone. Not just gone for the moment, but gone. Her things were gone. The sweet sense of comfort he felt when he came home now was gone with her.

His head wasn't clearer. It pounded. Ached. Along with his entire body.

But then, he'd known that would be the case. Everything he'd said to her was utter bull. He went to his bar and poured himself a shot of tequila. Perfect for doling out the punishment he so richly deserved. If he imbibed enough tonight he wouldn't be able to move in the morning. Maybe it would even trigger another migraine. All the better. It would cover up the real reason he was curled up on the floor writhing in pain.

He carried the glass into his room with him and slammed it on his bedside table.

He'd blamed her. He'd told her she didn't know what she was getting into, and it was true. That he couldn't be everything for her, and that was true, too.

But he'd lied when he'd said he didn't want to be her husband.

He did. More than anything, he wanted to be by her side all of his life. But how could he do that when he wasn't everything a husband should be? His father had been so strong and capable; he'd cared for them all. He'd made sure his mother was beneath his protection, always. And he, Eduardo, was so…so weak.

He had feet of clay and he feared one day they would crumble beneath him.

He lay down in his bed and put his hand over his eyes, trying to dull the ache in his chest, trying to staunch the sudden flood of emotions that was washing through him like an endless river of pain.

Yes, he would have his child. He was thankful for that. He would be the best father he could be. But he wouldn't force Hannah to be with him. She would thank him later.

Dios, but he wanted her. If only this could somehow be enough. If only caring for her would make him worthy of her. After all she'd been through, the disgusting living conditions and neglect…

She deserved more. A champion. For someone to come in and make her life easier, not harder. She deserved a man who could be a strong father to their child. A man who could be a capable husband. A strong businessman who didn't make mistakes.

He wanted to howl at the irony. He'd had it. Back when he'd first married her, he'd had that capability. To be the man she deserved. And he hadn't cared. He hadn't tried. And now he was hampered, hampered by an altered mind, and now that he cared desperately about being everything for her, about loving her as she deserved, he couldn't.

He reached out and fumbled for his tequila but couldn't quite grasp the glass. He shoved it off the nightstand and lay back, embracing the pounding migraine that was starting behind his eyes and stabbing deeper with each passing moment.

He focused on it. Reveled in it.

Because it took the edge off the unendurable pain in his heart.

CHAPTER FIFTEEN

AFTER spending the day locked in his penthouse, he'd called his driver and made plans to go to the ranch the next day. He wasn't in the right frame of mind to drive up to the house. His head was pounding and he felt slow and thick.

Then he'd called around and found out Hannah was staying at a luxury hotel. He hoped they had sheets with a suitable thread count.

The thought made his eyes sting.

They would work it out to the point where they would see each other. He would buy her a house, get everything set for the baby. That would be worse in some ways. Seeing her, being so close, and not being able to have her.

Because of his own weakness. His own fault.

He wanted to peel his head open and pull his brain out. Fix it, get a new one. He hated it. Hated the feeling that he was trapped. Limited.

Hated being without her even more than that, because he felt like he was missing something of himself.

Because something had changed since Hannah had come back into his life. He didn't want to be the man he'd been anymore. That man had been a fool. Arrogant. Selfish. He no longer missed him, no longer wished he could be him.

An empty realization since the man he was now couldn't give her what she needed, either.

He exited the penthouse and got into the black town car

that was idling against the curb. He rested his head against the back of the seat and concentrated on the pounding in his head.

The car pulled away from the street and out into the flow of traffic. It didn't take long to get out of the city and he felt the pain in his head lessen, even as the one in his chest got worse.

He looked up for the first time, his eyes clashing with the blue eyes of the driver, reflected by the rearview mirror.

"Have I been kidnapped?" he asked, his voice sounding hollow, shocked, even to his own ears.

"*Kidnapped* is a harsh word," she said. "I prefer to think of it as being commandeered."

"Is it any different?"

"A bit."

His stomach tightened down. "What is it you want, *querida?*"

"Me? A fair hearing. You don't just get to decide how things are going to be. Or did you not get the memo that marriage is a partnership?"

"I believe I decided we wouldn't have a marriage."

"Yes, well, I don't agree. And if I recall, when I tried to marry someone else, you very much didn't agree, either. You told me we were married and that was my tough luck. So guess what, Eduardo? We're married. Tough luck. That means we talk this through and you don't just mandate."

"What did you do with my driver?" he asked.

"I paid him off. I'm very wealthy, you know. And persuasive."

"Hannah…"

"Back to the subject at hand, though." She maneuvered the car off the rural road, into a little alcove and put it in Park, killing the engine.

She unbuckled and got out, coming around to his side of the car and opening the door.

"As I was saying, you don't get to make all of the decisions in this relationship. I want some say, too." She lowered herself to her knees in front of him. "I'm really hard to live with sometimes. I'm stubborn, and I can be materialistic, and selfish. Until recently I was afraid to care for anyone, afraid to feel anything, because I couldn't control feelings. But not anymore. And it's because of you that I'm not afraid now."

His mouth dried. "How did I…how did I make you not afraid?"

"Because you have accepted me. No matter where I was at. No matter what I said. You didn't let me push you away. You didn't make me feel ashamed for what I'd done, for my fears. You were just…there. No one, not in my whole life, has ever simply accepted me. Has ever stood by and supported me. But you have. You've done that."

"But…Hannah…I can't…I can't take care of you. I can't be everything that a husband should be to you. I'm… I make mistakes."

"Yeah, so do I. Remember the fraud?"

"You did what you had to do."

"I'm not perfect. And neither are you, but that's okay. I love you, Eduardo. And when everything else in this world fails, that's what will remain. It's what will matter."

He lowered his head, pain seizing his chest. "You can't love me."

"Let me tell you something, Señor Vega. I try to control and reason everything so that it fits my idea of perfection. From my sheets to my name, I try to make it all my vision for what life should be. I can't do that with you. You aren't reasonable or controllable or perfect. You're better than that. You're you. And it's those little imperfect bits of you that make you the man I want. I don't need to be taken care of…I just need a partner. And I want you to be him."

He unbuckled his seat belt and pulled Hannah into the car, onto his lap, holding her close. "Hannah, I want so much to… I want to be your champion. To make everything easier for you. I don't want to be a burden."

"Do you want to know something? When I saw you having your migraine…when I held you against me…that was when I realized that I could be a mother. Not because I feel even remotely maternal about you, but because I realized that loving someone, being surrounded by the person you love, was so much more important than status. Than things. I've spent all of my life trying to fill this emptiness in me. I tried to do it by just giving in to whatever I wanted anytime I wanted it. Then I tried to do it by controlling myself. Controlling everything I did. I filled the void with things. With a penthouse with a view. But the satisfaction didn't last. It wasn't real. The one thing I've never had is love. And you've given it to me. You've shown me not just how it feels to be loved, but how beautiful it is to love. Eduardo, loving you could never be a burden." She pressed a kiss to his lips. "I wish you could feel it."

"What?" he asked, his voice rough.

"I wish you could feel what I feel. I feel like my heart was trapped in a cage. I wouldn't let myself have emotions. I wouldn't let myself care for anyone too deeply, wouldn't let myself have friends. I was strangling my heart, suffocating it. And you set it free." He looked at her eyes, pale and filled with tears, so sincere. "I'm free."

Something broke open inside of him. A stone wall that had been wrapped tightly around him. And he felt it, too. Felt like he'd walked out of a prison cell and into the sunlight for the first time in years. She'd spoken of that feeling once, and he felt it now. So real, so intense.

His heart thundered, his hands shaking as he stroked her hair. "Hannah…I… You love me?"

"Yes."

"Me. This me. Not the me that I was?"

"Eduardo, this man, the one you are right now, is the man I fell for. You're the one who changed me."

A wave of relief, so strong, so powerful, washed over him. "You want me like this?"

"Yes. Just like this. I don't think you're diminished, or wrong, in any way. You're just you."

He closed his eyes and rested his forehead against hers, his headache fading. "With you, Hannah, I imagine maybe I can just be me. The me I am now. I was…as afraid as you were of changing back into who you used to be, I was afraid I never would. But I think we were both being stupid."

"Do you?"

He nodded. "Like our past was a destination we could so easily get to. Like it was one I might want to get to. I thought that by bringing you back, by seeing your face, I would see the past. But now when I look at you I only see my future. I love you, Hannah."

She smiled, real, happy. "You mean, you really do want to be my husband?"

"Forever. I was just…too afraid. Of failing you. Of failing our child. I want to give you everything, and I'm afraid that I'm so much less than what you deserve. But I don't despise the man I am now… I don't want to go back. How can I when you love me? When you'll be in my future?" He took her chin between his thumb and forefinger.

"I will be," she whispered. "I promise."

"Sometimes I'll have headaches. I'll forget things. I'll make mistakes. But one thing I promise never to forget is how much I love you."

Hannah smiled, her blue eyes filled with joy. "I won't be perfect, either, but I will be myself. I will be committed fully to you."

"I promise the same."

Hannah looked around them, at the mountains, at the car, at him, and she laughed. "It's like making marriage vows all over again."

"Only these are very real," he said.

She nodded. "From my heart, I promise, Eduardo. I'll love you always. You know…no one has ever loved me before. But you were worth the wait."

His chest expanded, his heart overflowing with emotion, with love. "Never doubt that I love you. I do. More than anything. And our children will love you. Our lives will be filled with it."

"I want that, very much."

"And you will have it, my love." He leaned in and kissed her forehead. "I never imagined I could deserve such a strong, beautiful woman as my wife."

"Some might say we deserve each other, Eduardo," she said, a wicked little smile curving her lips.

"True."

"And it's a good thing we're both strong."

"Why is that?"

She pressed a kiss to his lips. "So we can take care of each other."

EPILOGUE

HANNAH looked up at the picture that had hung in their bedroom for the past ten years. When she'd first seen it, she'd thought the woman standing in the crowd looked alone. For some reason, she didn't think so now.

Maybe because she never felt alone. Just as Eduardo had promised, her life was filled with love now.

She looked down at the nightstand and opened up the drawer, and looked down at the letter that was there, a blue ribbon wrapped around the outside. The letter from Benjamin Johnson, who was now eighteen and headed off to college. The letter that thanked her. For giving him life. For giving him his family. She smiled down at the paper, her heart swelling with love, and slid the drawer closed.

"Mama!"

She heard screaming and shouting and a scuffle, then Eduardo's deep voice scolding in Spanish and four sets of little feet running, then a door slamming. She laughed and turned away from the painting just as her husband came into the room.

"Everything well with the troops?"

"Graciela had Juanita's doll. And the boys were simply choosing sides to create a scene," he said. "I sent them out. It's a nice day."

She turned to him, leaned against his solid strength. "I need your quarterly report," she said.

He dipped his head and kissed her on the nose. "I already sent it to you."

She smiled up at her husband, the father of her children, her business partner. "Well, now I have no reason to punish you."

His eyebrows arched. "You sound disappointed."

"I am."

"Thank you," he said.

"For what?"

He wrapped his arms around Hannah and she rested her head on his chest. "For being my partner."

She went up on her toes and pressed a kiss to his neck. "Always."

* * * * *

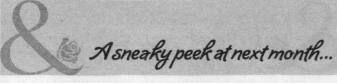